BEAUTY AND THE ROSE

A BEAUTY AND THE ROSE NOVEL

STASIA BLACK
LEE SAVINO

Copyright © 2020 by Stasia Black and Lee Savino

ISBN 13: 978-1-950097-46-3

All rights reserved. No part of this publication may be reproduced, distributed, or transmitted in any form or by any means, including photocopying, recording, or other electronic or mechanical methods, without the prior written permission of the publisher, except in the case of brief quotations embodied in critical reviews and certain other noncommercial uses permitted by copyright law.

This is a work of fiction. Similarities to real people, places, or events are entirely coincidental.

Cover design by Jay Aheer

Two Freebies!

Get these two exclusive books not available anywhere else ABSOLUTELY FREE when you subscribe to Lee Savino and Stasia Black's newsletter.

Sign-up on Lee's website to grab your free book.

PLEASE VISIT: WWW.LEESAVINO.COM

Sign-up for Stasia's newsletter to grab your free copy of *Indecent: a taboo proposal.*

PLEASE VISIT: BIT.LY/INDECENTSTASIABLACK

ONE

Daphne

I CAN'T BELIEVE we've come this far.

Logan clasps my hand as we walk through his flourishing rose-filled labyrinth to a fountain at the center I've never seen before.

It's springtime and I swear I've never appreciated the world sprouting new life with such fresh eyes before. Logan's hand isn't enough contact for me, though. I grasp his arm and giggle as we head toward the stone benches beside the sun-dappled fountain.

"I've never been so happy in my whole life," I sigh and lean my head against Logan's shoulder. His heat seeps into me and prickles rise on my skin. I'm so attuned to him. I never knew two people could be so in sync.

He bows towards me, his large hand finding my cheek and easing my face towards his. Our lips meet, gently at first, then with greater intensity. My nipples rise and arousal trickles through me.

I sigh into his mouth, "Logan." A prayer. A plea.

He wraps his arm around me and squeezes me tight—but not too tight. "I was so terrified I'd lose you." His voice is thick.

I press close, my chest grazing his as I lift my hands to his face. "You'll never lose me, Logan Wulfe. Nothing on this earth can part us."

I go up on my tiptoes to kiss him again, but right before our lips can make contact, out of nowhere—

"Wha—?" I cry out as the rosebush to my left suddenly shoots out a viney thorn branch that wraps around my neck.

Another shoots out and wraps around my torso, pinning my arms to my chest.

Before I know what's happening, I'm being yanked violently backwards away from Logan.

The thorns pierce my flesh and I scream in pain as I fly through the air.

Logan's mouth drops open and he lunges, reaching for me. I can see him fighting to get to me, but it's like there's an invisible barrier between us. And I know deep in my bones this is one battle he can't fight for me in spite of his incredible strength.

I reach for him, but more thorny branches pierce my skin.

"Please," I scream. "Not again!"

But I'm smothered as I'm yanked into the labyrinthine bushes and then swallowed up by the ground.

Buried alive.

I WAKE WITH A JOLT, wanting to scream. There's pain, everywhere in my body.

But around me, all I hear is the mundane hum of machines. The murmur of quiet voices in the distance. Before I open my eyes, I know where I am.

My lashes flutter. Each eyelid weighs a thousand pounds. My mouth is full of sand. When I lick my lips to wet them, the skin cracks. I hiss in pain.

There's an IV needle in my arms. White sheets tuck me into a medical bed. I'm surrounded by gray-blue walls with generic art hung here and there. Even the sunlight is dim and subdued, filtered through the thick glass.

The hospital. I've been here before. Too many times.

A chair creaks. Logan's sitting beside me, his huge body straining the limits of the poor hospital chair. He hasn't noticed I'm awake yet. His dark head is in his hands, his face bared. He's not hiding behind masks anymore.

I watch him for a moment, drinking in the sight of his large form in the Thinker's pose. He's a sculptor's wet dream. The muscles of his shoulders, the veins on his forearms—he's rolled up his shirt sleeves, the white fabric straining with the bulge of his biceps. The handsome slope of his jaw.

I must've made some sound, because he raises his head.

"Daphne," he murmurs.

I blink up at him. It's like whiplash, going from the dream that felt so real to this. We were just so happy, walking under the sunshine, it was only a moment ago...

But the monster always comes, doesn't it?

I'll never be able to escape. It was stupid to ever think I could.

I can calculate how long I've been here by the length of stubble on Logan's face. One, maybe two days?

I open my cracked lips. "Water..."

He offers me a cup with a straw and I sip gratefully.

Not so long ago, I cared for my father this same way. When he was on his deathbed. What goes around...

"Where?" I rasp as soon as I can get the word out.

"New Olympus General. The closest hospital to Thornhill was a shithole, so I had them medivac you here."

"Ah." I let my head roll on the pillow. I can imagine Logan yelling on the roof of a hospital, loud enough to be heard over the helicopter blades. I want to smile but the muscles of my face feel weak.

"How long?" I ask.

"You've been here thirty hours." He captures my hand and brings it to his face. I twitch a finger against his bristly jaw and find the strength to smile. None of this is his fault. He had no idea what he was getting into with me.

"You...need a shave."

"Daphne. Fuck." His big hands swallow my fragile one. For a moment he presses our twined fingers to his forehead, hiding his face behind our hands.

I swallow. The sand is mostly washed from my mouth. Time to ask the hard questions.

"How long?" I ask again.

He raises his head. His eyes are rimmed red. "I just told you—"

When I shake my head, he falls silent.

"How long...do I have left?"

He presses my hand to his face again. "The doctors...*fuck*." His voice is muffled. "They don't know. They say it's your third relapse."

"Yes." I remember the first two quite vividly.

"I read your medical history. Daphne..." He bows his head almost to the bed. His voice comes muffled. "Why didn't you *tell* me?"

I set my right hand on his head and stroke his thick hair.

Each movement is painful, like my very bones and blood protest.

"It was in remission." The inside of my mouth tastes bitter. I hate talking about my disease. My old adversary. So many battles lost and won. "I wanted to forget I was ever an invalid. I didn't want to live like that."

It's more than that, too, though I'm not even sure if I can explain it. I take another long sip of water before trying again. He deserves an explanation. "And it's like, when I'm healthy, I can forget this part of me even exists. Maybe it's a coping mechanism or maybe I really believed in my heart I was done with it."

Logan's face is still pained, though. "But everything that we did…everything I did…I *hurt* you, Daphne. The games we played…"

"No," I say fiercely. Is that what he's thinking? "I don't want you to ever regret our time together. I don't."

It doesn't take away the agony in his dark eyes. "What have I done to you?" he whispers.

"Not you. I was born this way." This was always my destiny. Doesn't he get that? The course of my life was written in my DNA before my heart's first beat.

Battleman's. The disease that took my mother's life. It lives in me now, waging war in a million of my cells. My body is a battlefield. It always was. And now I've gone and dragged the person I love most into the trenches with me.

I drop my head back to the pillow and close my eyes.

A male nurse comes in to fuss over me, and Logan retreats to the corner. I've had a thousand visits from nurses over my almost thirty years, but never with a dark presence brooding in the shadows. My skin prickles with awareness as the nurse checks my vitals, asks me questions, and prompts me to eat.

"She'll eat," Logan interjects, making the man jump. The nurse must have forgotten Logan, but I didn't. I feel Logan's gaze like a touch. "I'll make sure of it."

The nurse still has his hand on my bare back. Logan glares at it until the man snatches it away.

"The doctor will be in soon," the nurse assures me, and scuttles away.

"Did you have to scare the poor man?"

"He liked touching you." Logan prowls back to his seat by my bed. He carefully replaces my gown and plumps my pillows—all the little chores the nurse forgot in his rush to get away.

I laugh softly. As if anyone would want me like this, a frail bag of bones. "He's just doing his job." I sigh as I relax back onto the pillows.

Logan grunts but doesn't argue. He spends an inordinate amount of time smoothing my hair from my brow. His touch is featherlight on my forehead, brushing my hair back from my face, applying salve to my chapped lips.

The look on his face makes my breath catch. Concern mixed with tenderness mixed with heat. At least there's still one man who finds me attractive, even like this.

But when he leans down to press a soft kiss to my forehead, his lips are careful. Chaste.

"The hospital should hire you," I try to joke.

"Daphne." Logan looks more serious when he takes a seat. "I want to take over your treatment."

I blow out a breath. "I don't know if that's a good idea."

"Please, I'm close to a breakthrough. You've studied Battleman's, you know—"

"All my life. And I've gotten nowhere."

"You're close. I can take your research—"

"My father's research. The patents you stole—"

"It was my research from the start." He forces himself to lower his voice, visibly reining in his temper. "Look, I don't want to fight. I just want to get you well."

"It's like my mother and father all over again." Tears spill from my eyes.

"No. I'm not going to let you...fuck, please. You're not going to—" But he can't finish the sentence.

I look away from him and out the window, the grayscape hallowed in anemic light. "It was always going to be this way." And now I'm just supposed to accept that Logan is going to be a casualty with me?

"Don't say that—"

"Logan." Just a whisper is enough to make him fall silent. "This has always been my life. Every time I walked into the lab, I knew I was fighting for my right to live. For my next breath. Battleman's has been a part of me since I was a baby. If it wasn't for the disease, I wouldn't have even been born."

"What?" he asks, but he's smart enough to piece it together from what I'm saying. Stunned horror spreads across his face.

"It was my father's plan all along," I rasp. "He knew if they had a child, there was a good chance that child would carry the disease. My mother didn't want to have kids because of it."

Logan shifts in his seat and the chair groans like it's dying. Hospital furniture is way too rickety for a man of Logan's size—he could look at it the wrong way and it'd fall apart.

I want to make a joke to lighten the mood, but Logan's calling my name. "Daphne. Are you saying—"

"My father wanted a second chance to fight the disease. To harvest stem cells, run tests. To try new treatments." I push my cheeks up into a hollow smile. "He didn't want a child. He wanted a tissue donor."

Logan's broad chest rises and falls rapidly, his lungs like bellows. His left hand holds mine gently while his right fist presses against his mouth. "That fucking fuck," he growls, probably hoping his hand muffles the insult.

Now my smile is real. "That's my dad you're talking about," I say lightly. "Don't speak ill of the dead."

He lowers his fist. "If he wasn't dead, I'd kill him."

"It's done. It's past."

"Did he tell you? That you were only born as a guinea pig he could experiment on to save your mother?"

"Not in so many words. That would've made it easier."

Instead, my father's actions told me the truth. Every time he led me to his lab. Every time he threaded a needle in my vein to draw blood. Every time he injected me with a treatment that had a chance to heal me and my mother—*or* make me worse.

I learned my father loved me less than the results on a lab print out. Results he excitedly shared with my mother.

"Don't feel sorry for me, Logan. I had a better life than most. And my mother loved me. She was furious with my father for what he was doing. But most years, she was just too weak to stop it. And he hid the worst from her."

"I'm so sorry." Logan kneels next to the bed, gripping both my hands in his huge ones. His anger is still there, but he's pushed it to the back burner. "You have to know...you're not just a lab rat. You're more than what your father tried to make you. You're smart and perfect and beyond beautiful. You..." his voice chokes. "You are loved. So loved."

"I know I am." I stroke the raven-black hair from his

forehead, wanting so badly to kiss him. "As soon as I was old enough to realize what my father had done, I had you."

"What?"

"You were his student, so on fire. You said you were going to cure Battleman's." My voice softens. "And you were always kind to me. I was your teacher's skinny daughter. But you were still so nice."

"Daphne...I didn't know. I never even guessed you were sick."

"Oh I wasn't. Not at that point. The disease was in remission. Not because of the treatments—they all failed—but because my body was young and strong enough to fight." My father wanted to keep experimenting on me, see if he could poke the disease awake, but my mother wouldn't let him.

"You were my light in the darkness, Logan. My reason to live. Even before you knew my name."

But the nightmare feeling of thorns wrapping around my flesh and pulling me under the dirt flashes vividly through my head. Because I feel that darkness closing in around me again and it's so consuming I'm not sure even the most powerful love on earth could keep it at bay.

TWO

Logan

YOU WERE my light in the darkness. My reason to live. How can she say that to me, of all people?

I hold Daphne's hand long after she falls asleep. I have to be careful not to squeeze her fragile fingers too hard. When I finally lay her hand down, her skin looks so translucent, the blue veins are stark against the white sheets.

I've knelt for so long my bones protest as I rise. I grit my teeth. I've got to get out of this room, get some air. I hate to leave Daphne, but my stomach is still roiling from what she told me.

It was my father's plan all along. He knew...

What sort of sick fuck experiments on their own child? If he wasn't dead I would destroy him. Not just his company. They'd never find the bits of him I'd flay from his flesh. I'd lock Daphne in the castle for as long as it took for her to forgive me. After what he did, kidnapping her would be a mercy.

Guilt churns through me. For all my anger against her father, did I treat her any better? For all I know, my rough play weakened her and brought on this relapse.

I carefully shut the door to her private hospital room, just barely resisting the urge to slam my head repeatedly against the fake wood. Who the fuck am I kidding? I deserve to have the skin flayed from *my* back for what I did to her.

She was fragile and I spanked her. Made her stand in the corner once for hours. Made her crawl on the unsanitary floor...

My hands clench into fists so hard my nails tear at my palms. I'm a monster. Depraved through and through. My love is twisted. I unleashed all my demons on Daphne, made her pay the price of my obsession.

She'll never blame me. She's too good. Too forgiving. No, it's up to me to dole out punishment. I'll never forgive myself. I'll spend my whole life making it up to her. I'll cherish her and stay up day and night working until I find a cure.

Because even still, knowing all that I know now, I'm not giving her up. Even knowing she deserves so much better than me. The gods be damned if they think to take Daphne from me now. No. I won't let her die.

She won't escape me so easily. She'll have a long fucking life side-by-side with me until we're old and gray.

"Sir," the doctor touches my elbow. I whirl and growl. His hands fly up to show me he's not a threat. "Sorry," he squeaks.

"Shhh," I hush him harshly. "The patient is sleeping."

"I know, I was just—" The idiot goes to open the door anyway. To wake Daphne from her precious sleep.

I'm gonna kill this guy. He's gonna be a smear on the beige-tiled floor.

"Back the fuck off," I grab his name badge and stand to my full intimidating height. "Dr. Lockhart. Hematologist. Where exactly did you go to school?"

He babbles something and I sneer, releasing his badge. "Really? Not the butcher's shop up the street?" I grab the chart he's holding and scan it quickly, shoving him off balance when he grabs for it.

At the last second, my free hand fists his collar, keeping him upright. The man teeters before me, his Adam's apple bobbing as he swallows over and over.

"This is what you call a treatment plan?" I berate him. "You're barely treating her symptoms and aren't doing anything to address the disease itself. You don't know a damn thing about what you're doing!"

My eyes continue to scan the chart even though what I see makes my chest cinch tight. Her vitals are stable, but her blood cell counts are bad. The disease is ravaging her system. *Fuck.*

"Sir," snaps a woman in blue scrubs. She's Daphne's new nurse, a replacement for the male fuck they first sent. Her eyes are round but she's got her hand on the alarm button, ready to call security. "You need to let go of Dr. Lockhart. *Now.*"

I open my hand and Dr. Lockhart staggers backwards.

"Happy?" I ask the nurse.

"No." The woman meets my stare head on. "Your...the patient—is she your wife?"

No. Not yet.

"Yes," I say confidently. Because she will be. As soon as I can get the ring on her finger. "Her father just died, and her mother is gone. I'm her only kin."

"Well, visiting hours are over. She needs to get some sleep."

Visiting hours? They think I'm going to go home and leave the love of my life with these idiots? I exhale a growl and hold up Daphne's chart. "I'd like to go over her course of treatment." As in, I'd like to actually fucking develop one. "I'm a doctor."

"I understand, sir," the nurse says in a syrupy, condescending tone. "But your wife has been battling this disease since she was a girl. This isn't her first rodeo. We are the best hospital in New Olympus. You need to back off and let us do our jobs—"

Back *off*? Back off and watch my Daphne wither away and die in a hospital bed in this depressing as hell hospital? This is all bullshit. There are so many shady people on this earth and Daphne is one of the best. It's not fair that she—

"Fuck this," I roar, and topple a food cart. Both the nurse and doctor leap back as plates, trash, and trays clatter to the floor at their feet.

Before they can react, I spin and stride into Daphne's room. "I'm taking her out of here."

I ignore the frantic shouts behind me, "Sir! You can't do that. Sir!"

But they don't know what I'm capable of. I kidnapped her once and I'm doing it again. Right now.

I stand, brace myself, and all but bare my teeth at the doctor and nurse. "I'm her husband, her only living relative," I bellow. "And she's coming home with me right now. Don't dare get in my way."

I was worried about the slightest noise waking her earlier, but when I storm into her room, Daphne's all but dead to the world. It takes half a minute to rouse her.

The doctors hover anxiously in the background as I gently cup her face. "Want to go home, kitten?"

She nods, though it looks like it takes all her energy to do so. "Anywhere but here," she breathes out before her eyes flicker closed again.

It's enough for me and apparently it's enough consent for the doctors, too. They let me wheel her out to a private ambulance I arrange so I can take my beautiful Daphne home where she belongs.

THREE

Daphne

THE SCENT of roses is my first clue. And then there's the fresh air that tickles my nose, filling my lungs with sweetness. Outside birds are singing, the sound so loud, a window must be open.

Fresh air. Birdsong. Roses.

The hospital would never allow a window to open. So that means—

I'm not in a hospital anymore.

I open my eyes. The familiar sight of my castle bedroom greets me. For a moment, a burst of happiness rushes me.

Home. I'm home.

Until I realize that the room is only *mostly* familiar. There's no antique four poster bed. Instead, I'm in a hospital bed heaped with white pillows and surrounded by medical equipment, including an IV pole standing by.

It wasn't all a terrible nightmare. Battleman's is really back.

But as I blink more, I take in the Persian rug covering the floor that's always been there. The same bright sunlight, filtered through the same huge windows I've always loved. One of the windows is open at the bottom and birds hop on the sill just beyond the screen. No wonder I can hear them so well. I'm at the castle and the birds are singing.

A shadow falls across my bed and I startle.

"Daphne," Logan looms over me. He looks a thousand times better than when I last saw him kneeling by the hospital bed. He's clean-shaven and dressed in a crisp white shirt tailored to his wide shoulders. His voice is deep and soothing. "You're awake."

"Logan?"

"Shhh," he rubs salve on my lips. I can't stop myself from licking them—the salve tastes horrible but my lips are all healed. Logan tsks and reapplies the balm. "Are you cold? It got a little stuffy in here, so I opened a window. Spring's come early."

I blink at him, waiting for my thoughts to catch up. "You moved me?"

If I really think hard, I think I remember something about all the doctors gathered around and Logan telling me he was bringing me home. But it seems like a distant dream. I didn't necessarily think it was real at the time. I hate nothing more than hospitals, though, so I'm glad to be out of there.

And I'm with Logan and I love him and he loves me and we're home finally. Maybe it'll be different this time.

Maybe it's true what they say, and anything is possible as long as you have true love. I look at his beloved face, vulnerable and free of that terrible mask he used to wear.

We've come through so much. Can we make it through this, too?

"Mhhmm." He picks up a blood pressure cuff, fastens it around my arm, and takes my blood pressure like it's the most normal thing in the world for us to do together. I frown and my blood goes cold in a way that has nothing to do with my illness.

How many times did I witness this exact same scene play out? My father bent over my mother's hospital bed, set up in their bedroom? Taking her blood pressure, her temperature, or drawing blood. I've seen what it looks like when what was once love becomes clinical. How a series of triumphs and failures with every lab test can become an entire marriage.

Still, out of habit, I count the seconds along with him as the blood pressure cuff releases pressure.

When he finishes, he nods, removes the cuff, and leans in to kiss the top of my head—the *top* of my head mind you, *not* my lips—before going to the medical stand to enter the results on the computer. Then again, why *would* he want to kiss my lips when I've got this gross tasting salve on them? I can't even describe the despair that hits me at that thought. Because I can only imagine how terrible the rest of me looks.

From what I can see of the screen, all my medical records are there.

Logan moved me from the hospital. Permanently. Holy shit.

"Um, Logan...why did you move me?"

"The hospital and I had a difference of opinion on your course of treatment."

"A difference of opinion," I repeat.

"Yes. You know what? It's a little too breezy in here. I'm going to shut the window."

And he strolls away. Before he shuts the lower section,

he picks up a scoop from a big birdseed bag, opens the screen and empties the scoop on the sill. Then he removes the screen and closes the window. The sound of birds is muffled, but I see them fluttering to the sill to eat the seed.

The absurdity of it strikes me. Is this real? Do I really have birds chirping at my window like I'm in a Disney movie?

"Yeah." He answers, and I realize I said all that out loud. Logan straightens, a shy grin tugging the corner of his mouth. "I thought it might be nice for you to watch them. I ordered a few different feeders, but haven't had a chance to install them. Apparently different birds eat different kinds of seeds and—"

I squint at him. "Who are you and what did you do with Logan Wulfe?" Maybe it's not so surprising that Logan has a huge nurturing streak. He *is* a doctor. And he's just... *Logan*. The man who held me all night long when I grieved for my mother. The man who never pushed me before I was ready and when I was, guided me so carefully every step of the way.

"It's me, baby." His white teeth flash and heat streaks through me. It's weird to feel turned on in a hospital bed, but my body always reacts to Logan this way. I'm sick, not dead. "Are you feeling comfortable?"

I've been so busy processing my shock at my new surroundings, I forgot to assess the state of my body. I move my limbs tentatively. Less weakness than before.

"Um, yeah."

"Good." He settles into a chair at my side. One of the huge armchairs that's more of a throne. It's twin is gone from the usual place by the fireplace. That's not the only change—there's no fire lit in the grate, and there's a new flat screen TV that adorns the wall above the mantle.

Logan follows my gaze to the new flat screen. "I want to make sure you don't get bored."

"I can't believe you did all this. You moved me from the hospital."

I stare at the screen, still feeling too many emotions. I can't seem to settle on one before another is swooping in. Gratitude that he moved me. Anxiety. Fear. Love. So much love. Which makes the fear scarier than any I've ever felt before.

"No harm done. You slept through it, and through the night. I may have given you an extra dose of painkillers to make sure you didn't feel the transition."

"You're crazy."

"Yes," he agrees with no hesitation. "I'm going to get you well, Daphne."

My eyes start stinging. I blink them rapidly, turning my face away from Logan to hide my expression.

I know what's ahead of me. Endless tests, needles, charts. Days and nights in this bed where every second feels like a millennium. "I didn't want you to see me like this. Weak and pathetic."

I wanted to pretend...that there was a chance it wouldn't come back. That I'd actually beat this when I was a kid and wouldn't ever have to fight it again—

"Daphne—" I hear a rustle and then Logan's there standing by my side, his big hand sliding into my hair, coaxing me to face him. "Look at me."

My chest is filled with boulders. I want to turn away but he won't let me.

"Look at me," he commands, his voice deep and compelling. The timbre of The Master. His heavy brows oversee his stern expression, but his huge hands on my face are gentle. "You are not weak. I won't allow you to say or think that. Just look at your charts. What you went through, what you survived...and still you're full of love. Full of life."

I wet my lips. "I didn't want the disease to define me."

"It hasn't. And it won't." He looks so grim and determined, his huge form standing between me and death, I almost believe him.

But I'm done with fairy tales. I have to be. For my sanity. It's time for cold, hard facts.

"How is this going to work? Am I going to go through treatment—here?"

Logan tucks the blanket around me. "I'm starting you on a new treatment. An immunosuppressant. I think the traditional treatment is the wrong course of action. It assumes the deformed blood cells are the drivers of the disease. I think they're just a symptom."

Every blood film I've viewed dances in my head. Knowing the shape of diseased cells doesn't lessen the painful sensation in my body. It makes it worse. "But that's not the accepted model. My father—"

"Is gone. Maybe it's time to try a new way."

I'm blank-faced and blinking, thinking through the implications of what Logan just said. This would change the direction of my father's research—my research.

Logan leans down and touches his lips to mine, breaking the spell. "Trust me, Daphne."

But all I can think is—*he kissed me*. Where he was supposed to, on the *lips*.

His scent surrounds me, a crisp cocktail of his cologne and the clean delicious smell that's all him. "I'm going to heal you from this current relapse. And then I'm going to cure you."

"So arrogant," I whisper, but tingles run down my limbs at his proclamation.

Logan looks like a knight ready to slay a dragon. He cups my face, his shadow falling over me, his presence a comforting cage. I feel small and safe, tucked away in this room, hidden from the world, with Logan at my side to defend me from Death.

I want to close my eyes and give in to his strength. It would be so comforting to let someone else charge into the fight for me. To let Logan lead the front lines. To lay down the standard and *rest* for once in my life.

But as I look up at Logan, so confident and determined, I can't help wondering: is this what my father looked like when he made promises to my mother decades ago? When he swore he'd go to the ends of the earth, do *anything*, to make her better?

That lifelong battle destroyed my father. It eventually turned him into a monster and my mother and I had a front row seat.

How can I let the same tragedy play on repeat, this time starring Logan and myself?

I swore never to turn out like my parents, even before I knew the extent of my father's...betrayals. What he did to Logan.

"I just got you back," Logan murmurs, holding me even tighter. "I can't... I *won't* lose you."

They're words that are meant to soothe. Instead the uneasiness inside me grows, even as my eyes grow too heavy to stay open and I spiral back into sleep.

FOUR

Logan

I HURRY out the door before the delivery man can ring or bang the knocker.

They're delivering medical supplies, so you'd think they'd have a clue there might be sick people inside and they should be quiet. But the guy delivering equipment yesterday drove a truck so old, it backfired and woke Daphne up from a nap after it had taken her forever to fall asleep.

I about took the guy's head off.

I jog down the steps of the front porch to head off any calamities, but the van that pulls in is a sleek, new model that's so quiet, it has to be electric.

A man in a gray uniform pushes open the front door and I greet him. "Did everything go smoothly with the shipment? When you got it off the truck, was anything broken?"

"No, sir," says the man. *Paul*, by his name tag. "I double-checked everything myself."

I nod and follow him around to the back of the van and, after signing paperwork on the digital clipboard he hands to me, he opens the doors.

I pop open the top of the boxes and run my hands over the brand new, state-of-the-art hematology analyzer and cytology equipment. I've been waiting all week to get my hands on these. There are plenty of universities and labs that don't have such quality machines. But I don't care about cost. I'll spare no expense when it comes to Daphne's life.

I nod again. "They look like they're in good shape."

I'll be able to get much more accurate readings with this equipment and really be able to know if any changes we're making in Daphne's treatments are having even the most incremental effect.

"I'll use the dolly to get them safely inside," Paul says but I just wave him away. I don't want anyone else inside the house disturbing Daphne. She's the lightest sleeper these days.

"No need." I pick up the large hematology analyzer and heft it in my arms, then head for the door. Paul stands by, his mouth slightly open. He doesn't offer to carry the other box. A good idea since it probably weighs half as much as he does.

I'm quickly back for the second box anyway. It's heavier than the first but after a quick trip, I've deposited it inside as well and am sending Paul on his way.

It's another ordeal to get them downstairs and set up in the lab. I'm breaking a sweat by the time I'm done but it feels good. At least this is something tangible that I can *do*.

Better than sitting around all week watching Daphne suffer and not being able to do a damn thing to fix it.

I meant what I promised her. I'm going to cure her. I'll be strong enough for both of us.

She just has to trust me...

Like you *trusted* her?

My hands clench but then my cell phone starts blasting "Down with the Sickness" by Disturbed. I laugh out loud and immediately answer. "When did you change my ringtone?"

Daphne's wan voice answers, "You must be getting slow in your old age if you didn't notice me do it."

I've already started out of the lab and am halfway up the stairs. I treasure any time she's awake and hate to think of her ever lying there in bed all alone. At the same time, I feel the pressure beating at me from all sides. *Have to find a cure. Have to find a cure.* There's no time. Daphne's mother died young.

Even allowing the briefest thought spurs my feet faster and in no time, I'm pushing the door to Daphne's room open.

"How is my favorite—?" the words die in my throat, though, when I see Daphne spread out on the bed in nothing more than a slip of red lingerie. My mouth goes dry.

"Hi," she says shyly and wiggles her fingers at me in greeting.

"What are you doing?" I look around, immediately zeroing in on the open window. "Daphne, it's not safe. Your immune system is compromised right now and we can't take any chances." I rush over and shut the window with a harsh bang.

I turn around to head back to the bed so that I can cover Daphne with the thick comforter. But what I'm not prepared for is the fury on her face.

Or the pillow that comes zinging right at my head.

"Wha—?" I yelp before getting smacked right in the face by the pillow. I look at Daphne in bewilderment but she's just getting more ammunition, ready to launch pillow number two.

"Daph!"

She launches the pillow and I manage to get my arm up just in time to knock it out of the way as I stride toward the bed to head off any more attacks. They don't hurt, but she doesn't have the energy for this. She barely managed to get the second pillow the few feet away from the bed to even hit me, she's already that tired.

I sit on the bed beside her and grab her up in my arms. She struggles for the slightest bit before going slack.

"Don't you dare," she hisses. Apparently she hasn't completely given up the fight yet.

"Dare what?" I asked, genuinely fucking bewildered. "Usually I can follow your moods, babe, but you got even me stumped."

"My moods? My *moods*?"

I arch an eyebrow. "I feel like anywhere I step is a landmine."

She looks away from me, staring at the wall and biting her lip. So many times I've wished I could read her mind. If I could just see into that broiling brain of hers that's always ten steps ahead, maybe I could finally feel like I understand what's—

She suddenly looks back at me, a desperation in her eyes I've never seen from her before. "Make love to me."

Her words make me harden instantly. Because I'm a selfish fuckwit like that and I want her, all the time. Any way I can get her.

But I'm trying to be a better man. I peel her off of me. "Daph, no. We can't. You're way too tired for that."

"Says who? *You?* Suddenly you're inside my body and know what I can and cannot take?" She's challenging. Belligerent. Angry. And afraid.

Because underneath everything else, I see her fear. I see her vulnerability.

I might not understand everything that's going on in her head. Or hell, maybe I don't understand *anything* that's going on in her head.

But I can see she needs me right now. And I'll always give my Daphne everything she needs.

So I pull her against me and drop my lips to hers in the gentlest kiss imaginable. But Daphne's not having it.

She crushes her lips against mine and tears at my shirt. But it's like she barely has patience for that, only shoving it past my abs far enough so that she can get to my bare skin. And then so that she can get to the button on my jeans.

"Whoa whoa, Daph, maybe we should slow down?"

But she just grins up at me, the shadows under her eyes doing nothing to diminish her beauty.

She reaches into my pants and squeezes my ever-hardening length. "It doesn't feel like you want to slow down."

I groan and devour her lips, because I can't not. "You know that's not the problem," I murmur in her ear. "I'm trying to handle you with care."

"Don't." She leans up and bites my ear. "Just fuck me. Hard like I like it."

My cock lurches towards her like a heat seeking missile. Maybe if I'm extra careful... If I take it slow and watch her body for signals...

But slow is not on Daphne's radar tonight. She pushes me back on the bed—well, she applies the tiniest force to my chest and I go back because I know it's what she wants. And then, before I can consider anything else, she's climbing on top, straddling me.

"Daphne—"

But she silences me with a kiss. I'm not sure it's passionate, but it certainly is desperate. My Daphne is desperate and it fucking kills me.

So I kiss her back. In spite of the alarm bells going off in my head about how her being on top is the most taxing position for her, and how limited her energy levels are, and—

I wrap my arms around her to help hold her in place, and I kiss the woman I love back.

It's a shameful rush. Giving us what we both want so desperately, but in the back of my mind, a chorus of voices chant: *you're hurting her, you're hurting her, you're hurting her—*

I'm about to push her away when she suddenly collapses to the side, feebly reaching for her pillow.

"Daphne!" I exclaim, but she turns her face away from me.

"Go away," she says weakly into the pillow, still not letting me see her face.

"Daph, what the hell just happened?"

Finally she shoves the pillow to the side and glares at me. "I don't have enough fucking energy to seduce my fucking boyfriend, that's what."

First of all, her boyfriend? The term is ridiculous for what we are. And secondly, when did she get so foul-mouthed?

She turns her face away again. "I just keep sticking my foot in it. I didn't mean to say you're my boyfriend. I know we've never, like, defined things..." Her voice turns bitter. "Especially now that we can't even fuck."

This woman... I shake my head at her. Have I taught her

nothing? Then again, I've been so concerned with her external well-being that I've been neglecting the appetite I helped her develop. And sex was always the place where the two of us went to find clarity.

I lean over her and capture her wrists, pinning them on either side of her body. "I think you should take one of the sleeping pills the doctor prescribed tonight," I say in my lowest, most dangerous voice. It's the voice of the Master. "You'll need your rest for what I have planned for you tomorrow."

I'm hovering so close above her, I feel the shiver that runs through her body, head to toe. Even in the middle of everything she's going through, I can still affect her.

I want to curl myself behind her and clutch her to me, to prove to myself that she's real and she's not going anywhere.

But her needs come first and I need her anticipating tomorrow. Her life is in chaos and she needs order.

She needs her Master.

So I peel myself away from the bed and release her wrists. "Until tomorrow. Sleep now and sleep soundly."

FIVE

Daphne

I WAKE MIDMORNING, feeling refreshed for the first time in days. I actually *slept*. Soundly, the whole night through. Usually my sleep is full of nightmare terrors.

But last night?

Quiet. If I had dreams, I don't remember them.

Is that really his power over me? He orders me to sleep soundly...and I do? Or was it because I knew that behind those words, there would come *action*?

No more time to mull things over because there he is, pushing the door open with the morning breakfast tray.

But unlike normal, he doesn't set it up over my lap. He lays the tray on my nightstand and sits beside me on the bed.

Right beside me.

So close, I feel the blazing heat of his thigh against my side. It makes sparks zing elsewhere throughout my body.

They don't tell you this. But just because you're sick, it

doesn't mean the rest of your body just shuts off. Maybe if we were doing traditional chemotherapy... But we're not. And I feel just as needy as ever, maybe even more—but instead Logan's been pulling away.

There's just been so much distance between us. Even at a physical level. I've missed sleeping with him because I'm stuck on this narrow hospital bed. So much *distance*.

Until now.

What does this mean? Why is he suddenly being like this? Because of my pathetic attempts to seduce him yesterday?

Then again, maybe he's as hard up as I am.

"I can feel your thoughts spinning a million miles an hour." Logan looks down at me gravely. "It's time for all that to stop."

I squirm a little uneasily. "What's gotten into you?" I've gotten used to the easy banter between us. But Logan's not having any of it.

He leans over. He's not wearing the mask over the ruined half of his face anymore, but he's still every inch the Master. More than ever, maybe, because there's no obstruction to his ice blue eyes blazing into mine.

"I am Logan. But I'm also your Master. And it's time you remember that."

I reach up to caress his face but he catches my wrist in a firm grasp and stretches it over my head.

My breath hitches when I feel a soft leather cuff circle my wrist and cinch tight. I look up at Logan, at Master, but apparently I'm not going to have any control in this session. Because the next thing I know, he's coming at me with a sleeping mask. He settles it over my face, completely blocking out my vision.

"Relax," he intones in a low, mesmerizing voice. "Your

job is to keep every single muscle absolutely relaxed, no matter what I do to you. If you start to tense up, you'll be punished. And I promise you won't like my punishment."

Goosebumps prickle all over my body. I don't know about that, I've enjoyed his punishments in the past.

Within minutes, he has all four of my limbs tied down and with the distinctive noise of a scissor's *snip*, the filmy fabric of my nightgown comes away from my skin. I can't help gasping as my nipples pebble, not so much from the cold air as from his bold actions.

My stomach clenches and my toes curl in anticipation.

Master draws back. "What did I say about tensing your muscles?"

No, I wasn't, I was just— But I know better than to speak my paltry excuses out loud.

Will he punish me now? My heart rate speeds up and my thighs clench together.

A light *swat* hits my thighs, a switch from a leather riding crop? But it's nothing more than the barest stinging sensation before it's gone, the merest promise of a touch.

And then the Master's voice is in my ear. "The punishment will mean an automatic cooldown time period of five minutes every time you tense your muscles."

An achingly soft, featherlight touch that might actually be a...*feather* traces down the center of my chest and then up and around my breast.

I give into the sensation and gasp, "Are involuntary shudders allowed?"

He leans in again, the hot air of his breath tingling the hairs fluttering near my ear. "We'll take it on a case-by-case basis."

How can he make me want to laugh and go supernova at the same time? Not fair not fair not f—

"*Oooooohhh yes,*" the pleasured moan comes from a place deep inside of me, "please gods do that thing again with your fingers."

But his fingers are gone, as is the rest of him. Even his weight is gone from the bed.

I want to whine out my frustration. I didn't mean to tense up. You try having the sexiest man of your dreams in bed with his hands all over you and not 'tensing' with excitement. Ha. *Tense.* I'll show him tense.

I pull at the restraints on my wrists, but only lightly. I want as much energy as possible for whatever Logan has up his sleeve…whenever he actually gets to it.

But the next touch on my skin isn't a feather and it isn't a crop.

It's Logan's hands. I melt under his touch.

"Shhh," he says in his low, haunting voice. "No more play. You're mine and tonight we're both going to remember it."

He pulls the mask off my face and I'm met with his startling blue eyes, right as his hands come up to cup my face. But it's not like usual. He isn't holding my face so that he can lean in and kiss me.

No, it's like he's a blind man, trying to learn my face for the first time. His thumbs explore my nose, the shape of my eyebrow, the slope of my top lip, and then my bottom one. When I gasp, expecting him to slide his thumb inside my mouth, he only skirts along the open seam before dancing away to explore my jaw and the delicate place where it connects to my neck.

And the look on his face the entire time he does it—like he's awed. Like I'm a forbidden museum and he's finally allowed to touch the exhibit for the first time.

But no, it's so much more than that, because our eyes

are locked the entire time, and each external touch is connected to an internal touch, this zing of intimacy I didn't know could exist.

And my face is just the beginning. His exploratory massage continues down my neck, outwards to each shoulder, down my arms.

I've melted into the mattress at this point, but I don't want to miss a thing, so I keep my eyes drowsily open.

I swear though, if he does all this just to put me to bed, I'm going to kill him. If this turns out to be another soothing exercise to help Daphne sleep because she's too sick, that might actually fucking break me.

But then I see all sorts of implements on the table beside him in an open bag. There's the feather and the crop, yes. But also big fat candles with luxuriant looking wax. I've heard what these are for but obviously, never tried them for myself.

Master catches me looking and his eyes go dark.

"I want everything with you," I whisper.

I see the pain enter his eyes. Pain and indecision.

"No. Stop it. And don't look away." If my hands were free, I'd grab his face and force him to look at me. "I want *everything*."

But by his face, I see that he still doesn't understand. He still sees this, *me*, as something to fix.

"This is your fault, you know. You taught me how to want things, and now I do. I want the big life and I want you and I want kids—" his eyes go wide and shit, I didn't mean to say that, so I hurry on— "and I want...*everything*. I want an explosive sex life and decades under the sunshine." I look over his beloved face. "I want to grow old by your side."

He drops his big body to mine and cradles my face.

"You will. We will. I'll find a cure."

I shake my head. I'm not just looking for false platitudes. I know some people like to hear people say it's okay, that everything's going to be okay. But that's bullshit. There's no cure for this. My mom died. I watched her die.

"You're not listening," I say, exasperated. "You just want to fix, fix, fix."

"I'm going to," he asserts, as if there's no other possible outcome.

I sigh. Maybe that's how it has to be in his head. He literally can't fathom there being any other outcome. But that's a game I can't play. And I can't pretend for his sake. If I try, it will start to build up between us and Logan refuses to allow that so—

"I don't know what to do with you," I mutter, banging my head back against the pillow.

"Do nothing," he says, laying the whisper of a kiss across first one nipple and then the next. "Let me take care of all the *doing*. Lay back and let me give you a big life. Explosive sex. Let me make you want things and then give them to you."

I giggle at him repeating my words back to me verbatim. At least he's a good listener, even if he's ignoring the underlying gist of what I was saying and diving straight for the sex. Shocker.

"You think too much, little genius. No more thinking. No more talking. Give in. Relax your muscles or I stop. That's your only instruction."

A small part of me wants to balk. I want to keep arguing with him. I want to pick a fight and push him away.

"I want to fight the whole world," I whisper, a tear sliding out my eye. Embarrassed, I try to wipe it away but of course my hands are tied.

"Don't hide from me. Never hide from me," Logan says, eyes searching mine and seeing too much. "You want to fight, you fight me. You want to rage, you rage at me."

He disarms me with those few words.

I go limp on the bed, all my anger diffusing and running out of me like water out of a drying sponge. Wait, what? That's not how this works. Usually when I'm feeling bad, nothing can take away the anger. Except that it slowly fades into a gray depression.

But Logan's hands are on my body, massaging up and down. In non-erogenous areas, but then again, everywhere he touches seems to light up my body like a glow stick. And the last thing I'm feeling is depressed.

Finally, I do as my Master commands.

I stop thinking.

And it's so fucking glorious.

Quiet. The million racing, worried thoughts have finally quieted. There's a beautiful, crystal-clear silence in my head.

More tears spill out of my eyes, but this time they're from happiness. It feels good, so I obey his one order. I relax my entire body and struggle to keep it relaxed even as the Master begins his ministrations.

First comes a sharp prickle from the top part of my foot. I'm glad he didn't blindfold me again, because while most of the time I lie back with my eyes closed, focusing on the sensation, I like having the option of opening my eyes. I love to watch the intent look on Logan's face as he runs the object that looks like a poky pizza cutter up my leg, so slowly and with such intense concentration. Watching him is half the high.

Next he's back with the feather, but he stops soon when he sees that I can't help but tense up when it tickles me.

I can barely suppress my smile when he picks up one of the big wax candles. He sets it on the bed, then pulls off his shirt in that sexy way that men do, pulling from the back shoulders and tugging it off over his head. Liquid swoops through my stomach down to my sex at seeing his muscles and the dark trail of hair that leads between his sharply defined V.

He's usually so buttoned up, any chance seeing his skin feels like a treat. And to think, he's mine now. I can see this whenever I want. The giddy schoolgirl feeling is swept away by dread. *Until you get sicker and die.*

Nope. Brain turned off. Brain turned off.

I turn my eyes to the candle and train my eyes on the flame. But I'm greedy and I can only last a second before looking back to Logan. My Master.

He's watching the flame too. Or rather, he's watching the small puddle of wax that's slowly liquefying in the lip of the candle.

He holds out his forearm and drips wax in a line along the inside of his wrist where it's the most sensitive. I hold my breath, but when he doesn't react one way or the other, I burst out, "What does it feel like?"

His mouth quirks up on one side. "Curious, kitten?"

I nod, not trusting myself with words. Is he really serious? Are we still allowed to do things like this? Then I shake my head. Who the hell do I think I'm asking? Logan's a doctor and I've got my PhD and have spent my life studying this disease. If we don't know, who will?

Number one, there's no reason we shouldn't be able to, and number two, I'm not supposed to be thinking.

I trust Logan. For twenty minutes can I not just shut my freaking brain off and trust?

Even as I think it, my entire body relaxes. Logan and I

watched the candle burn and liquefy more wax until there's another little puddle.

Logan's eyes come to me. The hand not holding the candle massages my thigh, up and down, up and down.

"You'll have every experience this life has to offer," he promises. "Together, we'll explore every sensation, every feeling, every possible nerve ending of your entire body."

He leans in and breathes in my ear. "We'll have a lifetime of exploration. In sickness and in health. Together. Now close your eyes, and feel. Feel me and what I do to you."

I nod but I know I might disobey. He doesn't know how much I need this. *I* didn't know how much I needed this. And I will give myself to him body and soul... But I might peek.

I'll never give up looking at him now that he's unmasked himself. I need every line of connection possible between us and he's not stealing one of my senses. Not tonight anyway.

So I keep my body completely relaxed, but I watch. And he watches me watch, because he's constantly checking my face to catch my reactions. I know if I exhibit even the slightest expression of discomfort, he'll stop. But I don't want that. I want this moment of intimacy between us to continue and continue and continue, forever.

We've finally stripped down, and I don't mean just our clothes.

The first drop of the steaming wax on my right breast is a surprise. It stings for a moment but then just sinks into a lovely warmth that spreads across my entire breast. He avoided the nipple, maybe because it was also recently pierced, but he paints around the areola like a blood-red candle-wax crown.

Wax drips down the mountainsides of my breasts and I've never felt more...more fucking *alive*.

"There," he says with satisfaction, blowing on the hardening wax as it cools. "I've crowned you my Queen."

I might laugh if he wasn't simultaneously touching me and driving me absolutely crazy. He gave up on the PG zones of my body a while ago.

The hand not pouring wax is on an exploratory journey of its own.

"Ah ah ah," he chastises when I clench around his fingers buried in my cunt. "Relax or I stop."

No stopping. No stopping. But I don't beg out loud in case it makes him stop. Instead, I open my eyes and focus on Logan's face. The deep blue of his eyes. The furrow in his eyebrows when he focuses, and *gods*, how hot it is when his entire being is focused on bringing me to climax—

A warm wave washes outward with one strong, immense *pulse*. I don't know how else to describe it. It's unlike any orgasm I've had before. Usually it's intense and I'm clenching and chasing it and fighting and—

Oh shit here comes another one—

I meet Logan's eyes and see his wonder as he shares the moment with me, the second wash of bliss that has tears pouring out of my eyes.

It's so— So fucking *beautiful*—

He bows over me, face an inch from mine, but he doesn't kiss me.

He just keeps sharing the moment, fostering a crazier, deeper intimacy than I ever knew was even possible between two human beings.

"You," I finally whisper through choked breath, the tears still coming so thick. "The big life is here. I already have it. Right now. As long as I'm with you."

SIX

Daphne

TWO WEEKS LATER, it's a very different scene when Logan comes in the door. I'm already propped up in bed surrounded by pillows, scrolling through the day's news on my tablet. No longer cut off or disconnected from the world.

The curtains are thrown open wide and sunshine pours in through the glass, warming my face.

It's hard to describe the past two weeks. Physically, I feel like shit. But they've still been two of the happiest weeks of my life. Logan is doting but I call him out when he gets overbearing. I'm seeing a side of him I only had glimpses of before. He's kind and nurturing. A gentle giant. And he respects me enough not to cut me out of my own treatment process.

Like this morning, for example. He comes in carrying a stack of lab results, his brow furrowed.

"Are those from the experiments that ran overnight?" I reach for the papers.

Logan comes and sits beside me on the bed, not giving up the papers but holding them so that we can both look on.

"Your numbers are holding but we aren't getting the improvement that were looking for." His voice is gruff and I know he's trying to hide his frustration from me.

"We knew this might take some time." I interweave my fingers with his. "Cancer immunotherapy is still such a new field."

He frowns down at the papers. "Not that new. It's past time somebody figured this out."

I look at him fondly. "And that somebody is going to be you?"

He finally tears his eyes away from the numbers and he meets my gaze. "It's going to be us." Then he frowns when he sees my breakfast plate. "You didn't finish your eggs. You know you need your protein."

I stick my tongue out but reach for the second half of a boiled egg. "I miss greasy bacon," I moan.

"Eat all your grapefruit slices and blueberries, too. The antioxidants are good for you."

"Yes, mother." I pop a few blueberries into my mouth, just in time, too, because the next second I'm squealing as Logan jumps on top of me, knocking me backwards onto the bed. The papers go flying but Logan's focus is only on me.

"You've got a mouth on you this morning. Is somebody feeling frisky? Want to play?"

He reaches around and gives me a swift, sharp smack on the ass and I yelp, then giggle. I squirm for a second to try to get away from him but I don't have much energy and I don't really want to get away from him anyway so I tap out with my palm and call, "Uncle, uncle! I give in."

But Logan doesn't roll off of me immediately. Instead he

clutches me tighter and buries his nose in the crook of my neck and inhales.

"I love the way you smell," he says in a low rumble.

I giggle and try to push him away, to no avail. "You're weird."

"You're wonderful."

Full body happy sigh. Then I remember I'm sick and the shifting back and forth flood of emotions makes me feel a little tipsy. Blinding happiness. Followed by gut-clenching anxiety at the thought of losing it all and sadness at my day-to-day limitations. But then Logan touches me and all that fades away, and the joy is all I can see and feel.

Sometimes I think I'd pay any price, even Battleman's, if it means I get this time with him. And that makes me glad that life doesn't work like that. That there are no cosmic bargains to be made, no matter how many hours our puny little human brains waste coming up with scenario after scenario we'd prefer to our own.

"Okay, okay." I try to slide out from under Logan, putting my hands on his chest to show him I mean business. "I really do want to get some work done today."

His eyes are dark and hungry but like always, he accommodates my wishes and rolls off. Though not without one last lingering look and a growled promise of, "We'll pick this up later."

He starts to pick up the scattered papers but I wave a hand.

"What if we're too mired down in our thinking? Let's go back to basics. We're trying to create a living drug, right?"

Logan nods, sitting at the edge of the bed again while I scoot up into a sitting position. He helps arrange pillows behind my head so that I'm comfortable.

"Okay, so let's think it through. What are we trying to accomplish, at the core?"

"We need to create a modified T cell that's able to recognize the target," Logan says. "To recognize the diseased cells."

"Yes. And second, our drug needs to modify that cell in such a way that it replicates the superhero cell into a clone army."

Logan nods and starts ticking them off on his fingers. "Recognize, replicate. Third, it and its clones need to actually *work*, so it can kill the sick cells and not just be duds once they're actually injected in the body."

"And fourth and finally," I breathe out, "these magical cells we've treated to become super cells have to live for the lifetime of the person, so that it's a forever cure."

Logan waves a hand. "No big deal. We got this."

I laugh out loud, but there's a heavy dose of despair in it. "You know we've always had trouble with steps three and four. Belladonna's anti-aging cream work so well because we mastered the first two, targeting aged and diseased tissue and cloning regenerative cells."

"But we've yet to figure out a solution for delivering the super cells into the bloodstream in a way that allows them to live for the life of the patient, curing a disease like Battleman's long-term. I know, I know."

"I'm just trying to establish the basics. I can't help but think we need some new perspective. We need to think outside the box."

"Okaaaaaay," Logan says slowly. "Like what?"

I look towards the window in the sun and the bright sky. "I don't know yet. But I'm going to read and research and think until I figure it out."

Because one thing I have already figured out, with Logan's help?

There are two choices when faced with a life disaster like this: give into anger and despair or take the express train to acceptance and start fighting the hell back.

This is my life, dammit, and I will fight for every inch of ground I can get—and believe I deserve it.

SEVEN

Daphne

"YOU'RE sure you're ready for this?" Logan asks.

He's hovering again, a hulking shape in a custom-made tuxedo. The gold cufflinks, paisley bow tie and emerald green cummerbund at his waist does nothing to civilize him. He looks seconds away from brandishing a sword and rushing out to single-handedly defend the castle from raiders.

In a sense, the castle has been raided. By makeup artists and hairstylists, courtesy of Armand. He owns *Metamorphoses*, the top spa in New Olympus.

"I'm ready." I answer as soon as the eye makeup expert finishes my mascara. It's been a month and a half since I first relapsed and tonight is the opening event for The Healing Garden. The finishing touches have just been put on it and I can't wait to see. Adjacent to New Olympus General, and designed so hospital staff, patients, and guests can have a place to enjoy the fresh air and beauty of nature.

I feel giddy at the thought of finally getting out of the castle, even if it's still in a wheelchair.

I didn't know there were artists who specialized in just the eye area, but apparently there are. An hour with her and my thinning eyebrows are painted in. That was after she applied some sort of fast-acting growth serum to my lashes.

The make up artist shows me a mirror and my mouth falls open. My eyelashes look twice as long.

Logan isn't impressed. "I don't think this is a good idea."

"You can't hide me away in the castle forever."

"Yes, I can," Logan growls.

The makeup artist's eyes grow round. I thank her and she nods and backs away.

"Logan." I hold out my hand.

He's at my side in an instant, his big hand swallowing mine.

"You can't keep me here," I tell him. "It's not healthy."

"As your doctor, I disagree."

"I know. You've made that quite clear." I give a slight tug and he sinks into a chair beside me. I struggle with what I'm going to say next, but Logan waits patiently. "My father always wanted to hide my illness. It was important to him for me to hold up appearances, especially when investors started taking interest in Belladonna. He thought a sick daughter would tarnish Belladonna's image."

"Fuck that," Logan explodes. Rage ripples through his big body, but he keeps his grip gentle.

"Fuck him," he adds in a harsh whisper. "I'm not your father. I'm not hiding you away. I just want to keep you safe, make sure you don't relapse and... Fuck!"

He half turns away, his chest rising and falling so rapidly I fear for the seams of his bespoke suit.

"I know, I know," I soothe. I squeeze his hand, my grip

fragile as a newborn's. "I know you're not my father. And I'm no longer following that old script." The words are ashes on my tongue.

Every day I wonder if I'm going to fall back into the patterns I've lived out my whole life. Can I fight the disease and keep my new identity? Only time will tell.

I grab Logan's hand with both of mine. "Tell me what you're afraid of."

Logan brings my hands to his face, pressing his lips to my fingers. His answer is muffled. "I don't want to lose you."

My heart squeezes at his vulnerable tone. "My numbers are better, right?"

"Yes."

"So much so that when Cora called, asking if I could help with the Healing Garden, you said it would be okay."

"Yes." He's still not raised his head to meet my gaze.

"And I've been practicing. Going out to the greenhouse, going down to the gardens." Not that I've done so much as lift a spade or a hand trowel.

When Cora first called, she only wanted my advice on garden design. I poured over my mother's journals and crafted a proposal, excited for the distraction. I even donated several of my mother's hybrids to the cause. Planning a garden in my mother's memory gave my restless mind something to focus on.

And my numbers steadily improved each week, otherwise Logan would've ordered me to stop.

Tonight is the opening event.

"It's important for me to do this." I free my left hand so I can stroke his dark hair. "It's just a ribbon cutting. No heavy lifting required. I promise to let you know when I'm starting to get tired." I slide my fingers around his freshly-shaven jaw and lift his head. "This is important to me," I whisper.

"You're so brave." He's still not looking at me. "You amaze me."

"I amaze myself," I joke.

Despite my declarations, I fall asleep in the limo, waking only when the car stops. When I look out the tinted window at the crowds, I feel the first pang of dismay. Cora Ubeli knows how to attract free publicity. She's probably invited a bunch of movie stars and famous billionaires to ensure the garden gets as much press as possible.

Sure enough, there's a red carpet lined with paparazzi. Logan and I will have to run that gauntlet. My stomach flips.

Logan glowers at them. "Say the word, and we'll go right back home."

"No. I want to do this."

If not for me, then for all the Battleman's patients watching the news while waiting for their infusions. For the first time, they'll watch all the VIPs gliding down the red carpet and see one of their own.

Logan gets out first to assist the driver in getting my chair ready.

I smooth my skirt and straighten my silk blouse. The neckline is a little lower than I'm comfortable with, but the stylist assured me it was in vogue. The outfit is elegant and classy.

Even my wheelchair is fancy, a sleek, state of the art machine with heated seats, mecanum wheels and a rose gold finish. The control pad at my fingertips looks like it was designed by NASA. My wheelchair can't hover or shoot rockets, but I'm sure those features will be in the next upgrade.

It's important to me to be seen in public. I may be sick, but I'm still alive and fighting.

Logan parks my chair close by and opens my door. "Are you ready? We can still go back home."

"I'm doing this," I reply firmly. A reluctant grin tugs at the corner of his mouth.

"I thought you might say that." He lifts me easily and sets me in the chair. I fuss with my skirt as he dismisses the driver. A few photographers turned to investigate when Logan appeared. Now that I'm in my wheelchair, they raise their cameras.

I jerk up my chin. Logan's hand settles on my shoulder for a second. A reassuring squeeze, and he starts pushing me up the red carpet. I almost protest that I can wheel myself, but my arms are weak and wobbly.

I flinch at the first camera flash, but I don't look away. The red carpet stretches on forever, a gauntlet of glaring lights and black lenses. I force myself to curve my red lips and pretend to preen in the attention. I raise my hand and wave like a queen.

"Daphne Laurel—" a few reporters shout, waving for my attention. They shove microphones in my direction.

"It's *Doctor* Laurel. And no comment," Logan rumbles, and pushes me faster.

As soon as we get to the end of the red carpet and inside, my spine wilts. My forehead is sweaty from the heat of the lights. People are rushing to greet us. Above my head, Logan is rapping out orders, while I concentrate on staying upright and continuing to breathe.

After a moment, Logan quickly wheels me to the right, where an aide in a black suit leads us down a side hall to a set of elevators. I don't relax until Logan wheels me in and the doors shut. For a few seconds, we can hide.

Logan crouches before me and hands me an open bottle of water. I let the cool stream wet my throat, being careful not to rinse off any makeup. As much as I want to wash my face and admit defeat.

"My makeup is probably ruined."

"It's fine," Logan says curtly. His big form practically vibrates with tension. I know he's wishing he could go back and punch some of the reporters in the face.

My fingers find his. "Logan, I'm fine."

"You did good. My brave girl."

"Now I just have to get through the ribbon cutting." I stare at the lighted numbers signaling our climb to the rooftop garden.

Logan paces to the panel. He considers it a moment before he punches a button.

The elevator shudders to a stop.

"Logan! What are you doing?"

Logan turns and eyes me as if he didn't do something crazy, like stop a moving elevator. "Who did Cora invite to this?"

"You didn't check the guest list?"

"I've been preoccupied," he admits. And of course he has.

"Just a bunch of donor types," I answer. "Cora's friends. Why?"

"Not the Belladonna board?"

My heart melts. Logan's afraid for me. My self-appointed guardian. "Probably not. Even if she did invite them, it's fine."

"I won't let them bother you," he vows.

"I know." I force a smile. "Now come on. One hour, and we can go home. We can get through this."

He gives an unhappy grunt. "But do we have to?"

"It's important to Cora. She's a friend now. So it's

important to me. Just grin and bear it. Or... lie back and think of roses."

He studies me a moment. "I won't be thinking of roses," he says softly. "I'll be thinking of you."

He paces in front of me, hands in his pockets. The way he looks at me makes my pussy clench.

"Um, Logan?" I tilt my head towards the door.

"That's not what you call me," his deep voice rolls over me. My body quivers, attuning itself to Logan the Master. Just the sound of his commanding voice is enough to prime me.

"This is a scene?"

"It is now." He circles me, then crouches in front of me. He's so big, even kneeling before me he's still taller than me. "Part your legs, baby."

Yes! "Now?" My voice comes out breathy.

He raises a dark brow.

I slide my legs open. My skirt is so tight, they can't go far.

"Wider," he commands and I wriggle to pull the sheath skirt up. Logan watches me fight to obey him. I get the fabric bunched around my hips and push my knees wider.

He plants his hands on my knees, touching me like he owns me. Which he does.

Casually, he slides his right hand up my bare thigh. Eyes locked on mine, he reaches between my legs to stroke the gusset of my panties. I squirm.

"Be still," he orders. I grab the arm rests of my wheelchair, my knuckles whitening as I fight to obey his commands. My heart thumps like I'm running a race.

"You've been such a good girl," he croons, still caressing me. And suddenly I'm on the edge of orgasm. My pussy is purring, as if all these months of illness, she's been waiting, desperate for stimulation.

I half twist, rising up in the chair in an automatic attempt to avoid his touch. My arousal is on a hair-trigger. And Logan knows just where to pet me.

"Logan," I pant.

He stills his hand. No! So close! "That's not what you call me."

"Master, Master, please please please—"

"Come, sweetheart." His finger resumes brushing my pussy, butterfly light. Sensation knifes through me, snapping me in half. I bow over his arm, shaking as pleasure burns white hot.

I can barely whimper as Logan strokes me through the aftershocks, then takes out a crisp white handkerchief, removes my panties and cleans me up.

Dimly, I register him bringing the lacy scrap of my thong to his nose before making it disappear deep in his pockets. Twin red spots burn the tops of my cheeks.

He's going to make me go out and schmooze with New Olympus' richest without panties. I press my knees together.

"There," Logan says. He's not quite smiling but an air of satisfaction surrounds him like cologne. He presses a button and the elevator resumes it's smooth ascent. "Now I can grin and bear it."

LOGAN

I lurk on the edge of the garden, as far away from the milling crowd as I can get.

I glower like a brooding gargoyle at anyone who comes my way. People see my expression and detour to inflict their small talk on someone else.

I despise these sort of events, but it's worth it to watch Daphne blossom. She's lively and smiling in her wheelchair, sitting opposite Cora Ubeli at the very epicenter of the party. The wheelchair might as well be a throne.

She's so beautiful. Turns my heart. Every so often, she looks my direction and directs a dazzling smile my way.

It makes me want to throw her over my shoulder and drag her away from all these potential vipers. The Ubelis might be good people, but I'd toss any other one of these fuckers off the building with no regrets. I take my station of watch seriously. Nothing will happen to Daphne while she's away from home.

Home.

It still knocks me on my ass sometimes that I finally have one. Because of her. And I refuse to lose her, to death or any other damn thing.

Down on the flagstone courtyard, Cora Ubeli steps up onto a raised dais to make a speech. She is a striking, glittering woman dripping with jewels. There are many rumors about her rise to power at her husband's side, but people in Olympus learned early not to gossip about the King of the Underworld's beautiful new bride fairly early on after a couple of bloody spats.

Over the past decade, she's only solidified she has a right to her place by his side. She stands like a queen surveying her kingdom from the raised podium, and her voice is rich and welcoming when she begins to speak. Still there's an undertone of command that goes beyond polite matronly society.

"First of all, I want to thank Dr. Daphne Laurel, without whose research, none of this would be possible."

There's a scattering of applause and then Cora continues. She leans into the mic. "I knew I wanted to design a garden—a healing space where people could soak in fresh air and sunlight even while they're recovering. But it was only through my discussions with Dr. Laurel that I realized we could do something much more special. That we could educate as well as appreciate beauty. The plants here all have medicinal uses."

"For example, the yew tree," she points to a tree, "which is used to make a chemotherapy drug. And that's just one of the plants in this garden that is used to fight cancer. I encourage you to read the signs along the walkway and learn about the life saving properties in these humble flowers and plants. There are some amazing breakthroughs being made every day in some of the diseases that have plagued humanity the longest. Cancer. Autoimmune diseases. Even allergies."

The crowd smiles and nods along, completely with her.

"This Healing Garden is dedicated to one who lost her life in a battle against one such disease. Dr. Laurel's mother, Isabella."

Even from halfway across the space, I can see that Daphne's eyes are glistening.

And then Mrs. Ubeli calls Daphne up on stage to say a few words. I smile and clap harder than anyone there as my beautiful Daphne rolls up the ramp made especially for her as she ascends the dais beside Cora.

She's the only one I'm here for. Her and that smile on her face. I'll be forever grateful to Cora Ubeli for giving her this night. I thought all rich, powerful people were the scum of humanity but the Ubelis might just be one of the few exceptions. Then again, from the rumors I've heard, they don't exactly color inside the lines.

I'm still grinning, about to move closer in spite of my dislike of crowds—Daphne's voice is quieter than Cora's and I don't want to miss a word—when other voices filter in.

Loud, obnoxious voices from behind me. One in particular familiar loud, obnoxious voice.

"Phew, dodged a bullet with that one," Adam Archer says. "It's too bad, 'cause she's hot. But I could never have a wife who couldn't get on her hands and knees and suck me off at the end of a long day."

Some hearty laughs and other uncomfortable laughs follow his statement.

But I'm already swinging around, hands fisted.

They're only standing about five feet behind me, a group of three men, Adam their ringleader.

He smirks when he sees me coming. The son of a bitch.

I point a huge finger at him. He said those things on purpose, close enough so I'd hear him. "You're a dead man."

His smirk changes into an expression of fear far too late.

I'm already swinging for his perfect face.

EIGHT

Daphne

THE RIDE HOME from the Healing Garden is frosty. There's no other word for it.

Logan tried feebly to congratulate me on my speech and I snapped at him, "How would you know? You were too busy punching out Adam Archer to hear anything I said."

I couldn't believe my eyes when, during the middle of my prepared remarks about my mother's love of gardening and how much the beauty of nature reminded her that life was worth living—

Only to look up when there's a ruckus at the back of the seated area, and then to further realize that it's your current boyfriend punching out your ex-boyfriend and ruining *everything*.

"Look," he says gruffly, running a hand through his hair when the car pulls to a stop in the garage of the castle. "I'm sorry."

I barely contain my scoff but apparently not well enough because he asks, "What?"

Is he serious right now?

"They were two seconds away from calling the cops."

Logan's jaw flexes. "But they didn't."

My mouth drops open. Does he really think that makes it better? "Then what are you even sorry for? It doesn't sound like you feel like you have anything to feel sorry about."

Right now I really wish I could slam my way out of the car and storm up to my room...but humiliatingly, I have to wait for Logan to set up the ramp for me to get out of the van. Because this is how it will always be. Him waiting hand and foot on me and never listening to anything I say.

I knew we would get to this point. It's exhausting being a caretaker. He's too busy taking care of my physical needs to care about what I really *want*— He couldn't even care that I was excited about the garden.

More like he cares more about his revenge than he does about you.

He comes around the car, opens the door and sets up the ramp. But before I can roll down it, he drops his hands to both sides of the wheelchair and forces me to look him in the eye. "Look, I know I screwed up tonight. But I'm going to make it up to you. I swear."

Oh, Logan. He doesn't even get it. It's not about making it up to me. It's about letting go of the past so we can have a future.

I gave up everything. But he's obviously not willing to do the same.

I reach up and caress his face. "I'm tired, hon. Really tired. Can I just go sleep? We'll talk another time?"

It's not a lie. I'm exhausted after going out and then when Adam kept shouting for the authorities to be called after Marcus Ubeli's security finally pulled Logan off of him... There was blood running from Adam's nose. People were taking video with their phones. It was horrible. Normal stress is tiring, but *that*?

I need to sleep for about a week after that.

Logan continues staring at me, eyes searching mine, before finally nodding and pulling back. I wheel down the ramp and fifteen minutes later, I'm scrubbed clean of all my makeup and fast asleep.

A WEEK later and winter is still alive and well in our household even as spring begins to bloom outdoors. But there's little thaw between Logan and me. He tries and sometimes, halfheartedly, so do I.

We talk about the weather and politics and documentaries we watch together in the evenings...but that's it. The ground is too frozen to dig any deeper.

The garden party tired me out more than I expected... Or maybe it's everything with Logan. I don't know. All I know is that I've been less motivated to get out of bed. Logan asks me if I want to go down to the basement and work in the lab with him.

But the thought of hours working at his side, pretending everything's fine... It's no lie when I say I don't have the energy for it.

Maybe I was right, before, back when I shut out everything and everyone. Maybe I'm like my dad. He never had time for anyone, not even his family. He didn't even always have time for Mom, when she was the one he was supposedly trying to save.

It was probably idiotic to get my hopes up for more. No matter how amazing Logan is. Some circumstances are just too much.

He's too angry. Maybe if I was healthy, I'd have the energy to help him past it. But with me ill, every day is a reminder of my father and Adam, always in danger of another relapse that might take me from him...

I look out the window as clouds gather overhead for another springtime shower. Logan will never be rid of the anger. He'll never stop wanting revenge. Against the whole world if I die, no doubt.

Am I just supposed to live with my head in the sand about what's really going on? Am I supposed to just pretend that he loves me first above everything else when I know in my heart of hearts it's not true?

And how can I blame him? When I'm this...*thing*. I look down at myself, covered in blankets, not having showered in two days, and I think—

I think maybe he'll be better off when I'm gone.

Maybe then he'll have a chance.

I turn away from the window and bury my face in the pillow.

But right then the door bangs open and Logan stomps through. He's rarely one for stealth. "It's time for a bath."

I keep my eyes shut and pretend I'm asleep.

"You snore when you sleep so I know you're awake."

Then the covers are ripped off of me and my eyes jolt open. "Hey!"

"Up and at 'em," is all Logan says.

But when I still don't respond, he just starts to undress me like I'm a petulant child.

"What are you doing?" I yelp as he yanks my shirt off my head and then tugs the bottom of my sweatpants, tipping me backwards on the bed so that my head is hitting the pillow again.

I feel like a little kid being maneuvered by a giant. Two seconds later, my pants are off, and then my underwear and bra.

I cross my arms over my chest, covering my breasts, and glare at him. "I am not having sex with you after that."

For the first time since he's come in the room, I finally see a spark of emotion across his face. He grins at me. "Never say never. But like I said, we're heading for the bath."

And then, still not asking permission or waiting for me to agree, he hikes me up and over his shoulder, fireman carry style. My shrieks and yelps are ignored.

He takes me out the door, ignoring my own en suite bathroom and taking me across the hall to his larger jacuzzi tub, the jets already roiling. With no ceremony, he deposits me into the steaming water.

I make one last screech of protest, but then I sigh as the wave of hot water hits my body and starts to seep into my aching muscles.

And apparently it's bath time and a show, because as soon as Logan finishes dropping me in the water, he starts to undress. I can't take my eyes off the way the light hits his rippling muscles. His back is as broad as that of two lesser men. And the cut of his abs, leading down to that enticing V...

I yank my eyes away, but not before he notices where I was looking and snickers loudly.

"Like what you see?" he asks cockily.

I'll blame the flush of my cheeks on the hot water.

"No time for funny business, though," he says, much to my surprise. "We're here to get a job done."

Since when?

But then, heart sinking, I realize that I'm not the only one who's noticed the changes around here. Logan really isn't attracted to me anymore, is he?

I mean, he just tore off all my clothes, handled my naked body, and all he wants to do is...*bathe me?*

Oh gods, I must smell. That has to be it. He leaned in a little too close and got a whiff of Hermit Daphne's body funk. It was just one day I skipped my bath and it's not like I get that sweaty just sleeping, I didn't think that it would matter that much—

But Logan's already picked up a washrag and he's going to work with the efficiency of a practiced home care nurse. Washing underneath my arms. My feet. My back.

Because he's a loyal caretaker.

My head drops forward.

"Keep your head like that, I'm going to rinse your hair now."

Can I please sink down through all the floors of the castle into the belly of the earth and disappear now?

I keep my eyes squeezed shut and my mouth closed as Logan washes my hair, not even able to enjoy the sensation of his hands against my scalp, which is usually a highlight.

But unlike normal, he doesn't spend any extra time lathering my breasts and he barely skirts a fresh washrag between my legs before he's pulling the plug and letting all the water out.

Bathtime's over.

He didn't even get all the way in with me. He washed me from the outside of the tub, never even taking off his pants. And he's wearing nice ones like always.

He helps me out of the bath and towels me off with as much ruthless efficiency as he washed me. Apparently talking is overrated, too, because he doesn't say two words, even as he wraps me in my favorite fluffy purple robe.

He's not even trying to pretend this isn't our new normal anymore. Doctor and patient.

"I'm tired," I murmur. "I think I'll go back to bed now."

"What?" Logan asks with alarm he tugs on a crisp, white shirt and starts to button it. "But now we can go down for lunch."

I sigh. "I really don't feel up for it. Can't you just bring me up a plate later?"

His eyebrows drop low, signaling his alarm. "No, I can't just bring it up later. I worked hard putting together the meal. For you. You need to be there."

Extra long sigh. Why are we even pretending anymore? I'm too tired for any of this.

But Logan suddenly pulls me forward into his arms and presses a hard kiss against my forehead. "We are going to be okay, you and me. And that starts today. Please," he whispers, "come downstairs. I know I fuck things up sometimes. But I want to make it better. I love you."

His words split my hard façade straight down the middle and I start to shake.

No. I have to be strong. I can't let myself get pulled in by beautiful words because the next disappointment will only hurt that much more.

And yet still, I nod when he holds out his arms for me. He ignores any uncertainty and helps me pull on a yellow sundress over my head. I'm surprised he bothers because I've barely worn anything other than a robe or PJs since coming home from the hospital. But maybe he thinks getting dressed will brighten my mood. Fat chance. Still, it does feel nice as he combs out my long, dark hair.

And afterwards, when he sweeps me up in his arms and carries me downstairs, I sink against his chest. I lean my head on his shoulder and listen to the comforting *thump thump thump* of his heart by my ear.

Why can't things always be simple like this? I close my eyes and luxuriate in the feeling of his strong, protective arms around me. I miss the pretending. I miss the illusion that he could love me more than anything else and the idea that he would fight anything, even his lesser nature, because of that love.

But maybe that was always a fairytale. And maybe I should learn how to be happy with what I have, because even if it's not perfect, it's still pretty damn amazing. I'm not perfect. Why should I expect him to be?

I nuzzle my face in that spot I love between his neck and shoulder and inhale. I'm just so mixed up about everything. I don't know which emotions to trust anymore. I wish there was someone to talk to about all this, someone who could help me see clearly and make sense of things—

But just then, I feel a *whoosh* and then the breeze on my face as Logan opens a door.

I pull my face out of his neck and look up right as a group of people start cheering and whistling.

What the hell—?

I can't look enough places at once. The backyard has been transformed. There are lines of chairs and all of them are filled with people. Glittering, beautiful people, dressed to the nines. It's like a redo of the garden party, everyone who is anyone is here, including the Ubelis and a grinning Armand, and there's an— There's an—

An *AISLE* down the center of the chairs, covered in rose petals, and at the front—

I swing my head up to Logan, who's still holding me in his freaking arms like I'm a damsel in distress, my hair still damp from my bath earlier—

But he's grinning as wide as anyone I've ever seen.

"Surprise, gorgeous. Welcome to your wedding."

NINE

Daphne

"TAKE. ME. BACK. INSIDE," I hiss up at Logan, turning my head to look away from everyone gathered in front of the garden.

Was I not sick enough? Now he's trying to make me die of humiliation?

Logan, smart man that he is, promptly turns around and carries me back inside. I don't take a full breath until I hear the door close behind us, but not before I register the chatter start up in the garden beyond.

I would so kill Logan right now if I had the energy.

"Put me down." It's taking everything I have in me not to lose my shit on him. What was he thinki—?

He lays me tenderly on the couch and watches me with an unreadable expression. But he certainly doesn't look contrite.

Does he actually think this is okay?

"You can't just order me to marry you!" I toss my hands

up. After all this time, does he still not get it? "You're my master in the bedroom, not my life."

But all he says is, "You don't want to marry me?" He watches me with seductive, dangerous eyes.

A pain twists my guts. I look away. That's not fair. I don't know what else to say but, "Not like this."

He nods and turns away, walking to a window that looks out on the back garden. "You told me this was what you always wanted."

I can feel my face scrunch in confusion.

He waves to the window and the labyrinth garden beyond. "A wedding like your mother's. A garden. All your friends." Then he comes over and crouches in front of me. "And I promised to make all your dreams come true."

He's trying to be sweet but he's only making it worse.

He didn't say anything about love.

This is just another way he's trying to take care of me. It's like that Cancer Wish foundation for little kids, except for grown-ups. He thinks this is what I always wanted, so he's trying to give it to me before I... Before I...

I can't help the little cry of anguish at the thought of the pity wedding everyone's thrown together for me.

And I'm sorry, but no matter how much I love them all, I can't go through with the farce. I can't be the good little bride like my mother was.

I can't pretend that someday Logan's devotion won't turn sour. Those flowers out back will wilt, and all that's beautiful about our love will turn ugly and destructive.

"No."

I look up in confusion at Logan's declarative statement. "What?"

"No to whatever is going on in that head of yours."

"You don't know what I'm—"

"You don't want to get married today, fine. But I'm done with this bullshit between us." He makes a decisive swiping motion with his hand.

"I don't know what you're talking about—"

He pulls his cell out of his pocket and hits a button. "Hey Armand. Yeah, the wedding's off. No, no, Daphne is just not feeling up to it today. She's fine. I promise. We just need to postpone for a few weeks."

Logan ignores my indignant scoff and the daggers I'm shooting his way. He smiles and chuckles and says, "Yep." And then a few seconds later, "Yep." And then. "Will do. Talk soon." Then he hangs up the phone and turns back to me like he hasn't been secretly collaborating with one of my friends behind my back.

I open my mouth to confront him but he's already talking. "Now," he puts a fist to his chin. "What are we going to do with *you*?"

I can't help the outraged noise that escaped my throat. "Nothing. You aren't going to do anything about me because you aren't the boss of me."

A dark light enters his eyes and burns with intensity. "Aren't I? In the bedroom at least? Even you admitted I was Master there."

My mouth drops open. "I— That was— You're taking everything out of context!"

"Am I? Or am I just finally starting to make a helluva lot of sense?" Logan grins at me.

Then he picks me up and hauls me off to the bedroom.

I squeal and, as he slams the bedroom door shut behind him, protest, "Logan, we can't! All our friends are downstairs."

"There's no Logan here," is his calm response. "The Master is in. And kitten, you've been a bad girl."

TEN

Logan

"TAKE off your robe and lie down on the bed," I order.

Daphne's eyes are wide, but as I face her and cross my arms over my bare chest, my Resting Dom Face firmly in place, her body relaxes.

I don't know if she realizes how much she responds to my commands. Her gaze lowers and the tension flows out of her body. Her shoulders soften and her movements become slow and graceful, more languid as she harnesses her incredible intelligence and focuses on obeying me.

The way she responds makes me feel ten feet tall. I fall into my own headspace, that godlike realm of the Dom where I notice every wrinkle on her brow, every microexpression and eyelash flutter, every flinch and every excited tremor. I see everything and everything I see, my entire world, is Daphne.

This is good for us. Maybe it's time to impose more

rules. Power exchange, twenty four seven, three sixty five. The thought is very tempting.

But there's a reason I've been taking it easy on her. Holding myself back. Even though I just saw her naked in the bath, when she drops the robe, I internally wince at how thin she's become. How frail. Not that she isn't beautiful as ever, but the disease has ravaged her body.

The beast inside me calms. Turns from a violent predator ready to wreak its will and wreck his prey—in the best way—into a gentle lion. I still hold all the power—the control Daphne gives me—and I will use it to protect and care for her.

But she still needs to know she belongs to me.

"You've forgotten who's in control," I say as I gather her damp hair and braid it so it's out of the way. She lies on the bed as ordered and the only sign she's disturbed is the rapid rise and fall of her chest. I splay a hand over her collarbone, between her breasts. "I'm going to remind you. Breathe, Daphne."

I coach her to breathe deeper and deeper, my voice low and patient. After a few minutes, I take my hand away, and she continues breathing slowly into her diaphragm. Her eyes are half closed, but I cover them with a blindfold anyway.

"You'll see what I want you to see," I say when she makes a small noise of protest. "You'll move when I tell you to move. Right now I want you to relax and focus on your breath."

I pause a moment to watch her obey. Even more slender than usual, Daphne is stunning. Her dark hair contrasts with her ivory smooth skin. Her lips are pursed in a way that tells me she's annoyed at the blindfold. The blindfold chafes me more than it does her. Covering her lovely green eyes should be a crime.

I slide a box out from under the bed and contemplate my options. The rope I disregard. Even though it's gentle and soft, I don't feel like restraining her. The nipple clamps will also remain in their fancy wooden box.

Instead, I grab a black box that holds several vials of oil. I pour the contents of the first bottle onto my palms and rub them together briskly to warm them up.

Daphne's skin is petal soft. The final bits of tension ease out of her as I squeeze her shoulders, massaging carefully. Her limbs seem so tiny and fragile, like a bird's. My hands warm her flesh as they rub every inch, reacquainting themselves with her body, every curve and hollow.

Well, almost every inch. When I reach her pussy, I pass by it, massaging down her legs. I spend a long time rubbing her feet, enjoying the way she coos. But even while she's ooohhhing and aaahhing, her hips are riding up as if to present her pussy.

I stop massaging abruptly and slide a pillow under her hips, propping her up. She lies there, waiting, offering up her sex.

I reach for the black box again. This time, I select an oil that should make her extra sensitive. The kind I paint carefully onto her labia, using a thick brush. With every pass, her hips tighten further, until she's rocking subtly upwards.

"Logan," she moans as the bristles stroke her sex. "Please touch me."

I say nothing.

"Master," she whispers, then clears her throat and tries again. "Master, please."

"You want me to touch you?" I set aside the vial and the brush, and lay a hand on her midriff. "Here?"

"No. Lower..."

"Oh, kitten, you have to earn that." I go back to massaging her sides, even the taut globes of her ass. Being careful not to touch the parts of her I used the special oil on.

I can tell the moment that oil starts working, because a low moan starts in her throat. It grows louder, and pauses as she realizes she's making a sound. Then it continues. Her hips are full out rocking now, and her hands are curled into fists at her sides. As I watch, she makes to touch her pussy—

"No," I thunder. She freezes and I continue in a softer tone, "No touching. I will tie you down."

She lasts another minute with her hands fisted at her sides. Her poor neglected pussy is slick and puffy, arousal turning the shell-like folds a deep rose.

I'm a sadist, so I smile as I watch her squirm. "Want some relief?"

She nods frantically.

"I'm going to let you earn your reward." I remove my jeans and kneel on the bed, up beside her head. "Make me feel good."

I straddle her head and carefully feed her my cock. If her health was back to a hundred percent, I'd face fuck her. And make her hold a vibrator to her clit, and punish her when she grew distracted by her own arousal. I'd make her practice until she could suck me perfectly.

Something to look forward to.

This time I make her do the work, looking down at her as she cranes her head to bob up and down on my cock. She transforms her driving need into a desire to please me, and I revel in her abject service. Until she swallows me so far down she gags.

"Slowly, sweetheart," I lean back. The pained, eager

noises escaping her throat make my cock jerk. She's not the only one aching to cum.

"You want me to fuck you?"

She nods with my cock still in her mouth.

I pull out of her mouth, even though my balls are screaming for release. "Maybe later. If you're good."

I slide off the bed and go back to massaging her tense body. This time it does nothing to calm her. Grinning, I lean close and blow on her sex.

"Uhn, Logan, it's too much!"

"Poor baby." I'm hard as a steel pipe. It's hard to walk away from the bed back to my box of toys, but I manage. Her head snaps my direction when I turn on the vibrator.

"Let's see how much you can take."

She whimpers when I order her not to cum, but she still does her best. I take pity on her, somewhat, and start on the lowest setting. But I don't keep it there for long. I slowly increase the tempo of the vibrations, until her breath comes in shocked hitches, until a deep flush roams down the valley between her breasts.

"Please," she whispers, and it becomes a chant. "Please, please, please." She's so close, her toes are curling and her head thrashes back and forth.

I toss the vibrator away and mount her. There's a slight tingle on my cock as the oil coats it. Worth it to sink balls deep inside her.

Daphne sighs and clamps her legs around me. Her pussy clamps on my cock.

I pull the blindfold off. The half-hazy, half-frantic look in her eyes almost sets me off. I cup her face and kiss her, drinking deep of her until I'm lost in her mouth.

I grip her hair and break away. A sweat breaks out over

me as I slowly dip in and out of her sweet channel. We're face to face, so close our breath mingles.

"You will marry me. One day," I vow.

Her lips part but she doesn't say anything. Her eyes are unfocused, so I wait for her to return to me, continuing to ease out and in of the perfection of her body.

She winds a hand around my neck, her nails biting my skin. I pull all the way out and slam back into her, making us both groan. My orgasm rises, a great rush of pleasure spreading its wings over me and I thrust faster and faster, chasing it. Daphne's channel squeezes my cock, impossibly tight. Any tighter and we'll be joined forever.

"Next time you'll say yes," I pant in her ear.

She's breathless but pert as she retorts, "Next time, you should actually ask."

I speed my thrusts and our laughter turns to gasps. We're still smiling as we go over together.

ELEVEN

Daphne

I'M IN DREAMLAND, riding a wooden horse while wearing a huge white dress, frantically trying to get to Logan so I can marry him—but every time he comes into view, the Merry-Go-Round swings me away before I can say 'I do.'

Then "Mambo No. 5" breaks into my dream and shatters it, pulling me awake.

I roll over and grab my phone, answering it with a half audible, "Hello?"

"Daphne, darling, how are you?" Armand trills in my ear. "Did I wake you?"

"It's okay." I push my hair back from my face. Yesterday I left Logan at the altar. But not really, since he never asked me to marry him in the first place. Compounded by the awkwardness of him inviting all our friends. We made up but I still haven't dealt with the fallout.

Armand is prattling in my ear like it never happened.

"I'm calling to share the good news, darling. I'm expanding into New Rome, opening seven new locations."

I make appropriate happy noises. I'm still waking up.

"I have a new investor. Just listen to his name: Sebastian St. James. Doesn't it just scream wealth and power?"

I murmur my agreement, but I only understand half of what he's saying.

"I nearly swooned when I met him," Armand continues. "So stern and handsome. But young." A pause, and then he adds, "You must meet him."

"Uh, no," I say quickly. Is Armand seriously matchmaking right now? "I think I'm good with the one I got."

"Are you now?" Armand's tone is so offhand, I know he's super interested.

"Yes. Definitely. Logan is the man for me. Speaking of which," I close my eyes as my stomach knots in embarrassment. "Uh, I'm sorry you came to my wedding…and it never happened."

"It's no problem, girl. I'm always happy to plan a wedding."

I wince. I hadn't realize he'd planned the whole thing. When I say so, he laughs.

"Your wedding, when it happens, will be the event of the year. I will make it so."

"Uhh, thanks," I make a mental note to elope if I ever want to say 'I do.' "Is Cora mad? She and her husband came all this way, and—"

"Don't worry about that. Cora of all people understands what it's like to be held captive by the man you love," he says, which is not really an answer.

I frown into the phone. "Logan isn't holding me captive."

"Isn't he?"

"All right, sorta. But...he isn't holding me against my will." Not really. Not any more. "He didn't capture me. He saved me."

There's a long silence where he digests my words, and I feel relief at the life I escaped. I'm not CEO of my father's company anymore, and so much has changed, but at least I'm living life on my terms.

"How are you feeling?"

"Better. It's one day at a time. Tell me more about your new spa." He happily changes the subject and we chat easily for a few more minutes. He jokes a few more times about planning my wedding as the "event of a lifetime."

I end the call and droop against my pillows, wondering if I can borrow his certainty about my future. There's no way I can marry Logan when I know I'm dying. I won't shackle him to me, and he won't let me go.

Only one thing to do, I tell myself as I rise out of bed, hobbling towards the bathroom to start my day. *Keep moving forward. Don't waste a minute.*

We will find a cure. We have to.

LOGAN

"Good morning, dove," Daphne calls out in a singsong as her chair finishes riding on the track I installed down the wall of stairs.

I look up from the microscope. I didn't know she was awake yet.

My breath catches for a moment. She's so beautiful. She's finally started putting on more weight again, even if just the slightest bit. I'm constantly trying to get her to eat more. But she just doesn't have much of an appetite.

I would have been far happier simply carrying her down and up the stairs every day but her independence is important to her. And what's important to her is important to me. I get it, I do. When I was stuck in that hospital, I hated having to wait for someone to bow and scrape for my every need.

But those were strangers. This is me. It's been a hard lesson to learn. But we're getting there.

"What are you working on?" She rolls over to my side and immediately her hand comes to my bare forearm where I rolled my sleeves up. I love that the second she sees me, it's unconscious, she has to touch me. Reestablish contact. I cover her hand with my own and squeeze.

With a single touch, my tether to this world comes back into focus. I will be strong, for her.

"Same old, same old. The super T cells we treat with the rose essence colonize well enough in the petri dishes, but the ones that survive reentry into the body and start replicating just don't last that long."

She nods. This is the problem that we've been facing for weeks now. She wheels her chair over to the microscope where I'm working. I step aside and she fits her eyes to the sights. "At least it's latching onto the Battleman's antigen cells. We've got our targeting spot on."

What does that matter, if we can't deliver it into the body where it's needed? I want to shout. But no, I never show my frustrations in front of her. I was selfish for too long. No more. Daphne's going to get the version of Logan she should have gotten all along.

"Little by little," I say.

"We learn the alphabet," she finishes the saying for me.

We picked up a book of foreign euphemisms and they've become our inside jokes. The Romanian rhyme about keeping on, keeping on had landed close to home with both of us.

She joins me by my side and we do exactly as we said, little by little. Doing the work of research scientists. It's far from glorious. We make incremental changes and test. Experiment after experiment. Some fail, some show promise. More incremental changes. More testing.

We'd be down in this airless basement for days on end if I let us. So it's always me keeping my eye on the clock and dragging an always tired Daphne away from her work. To eat. For her mandatory afternoon nap.

Even when she's obviously run ragged, she refuses to acknowledge her own limits. I want to throttle her for not protecting herself and at the same time I want to wrap her in so many blankets and put her on a pedestal where no one can touch her and nothing bad could ever happen to her.

I'm always fighting two wars—against the actual disease and against Daphne's stubbornness. She's determined to have her big life, now. And I want to give it to her... As long as it doesn't interfere with her long-term recovery. Something she can lose sight of in the moment when she's lost in research or lost in my body.

And we are having so much sex. Every night, that's a given. No matter how tired she is, she begs me to take her. Sometimes that means getting creative with how the pillows are arranged so she can just lay back and let me do the heavy lifting. Other times it means tying her down to the bed so tight she couldn't twitch a muscle even if she wanted to.

So, we're managing to figure it out...

But for how long? That's the thought that keeps me

awake at fucking night. Everything's too good right now. And in my life, nothing good ever lasts.

"Logan? Logan?"

My head jerks up and I look her direction. "What?"

Daphne looks at me quizzically. "I asked if you were done with that sample." She reaches out a gloved hand.

"Oh, right." I take the slide off of the microscope I'm looking at and hand it over to her.

She slips it into her machine and is immediately intent, examining it through the illuminated scope. She shakes her head, watching the same drama I watched a hundred times as it plays out. Our super T cell is introduced into a colony of diseased Battleman's cells.

While our super T cell begins to attack the diseased cells, it simply doesn't have staying power. It clones itself a few times but then all the clones die and the Battleman's continues to torture for another day.

I don't know how Daphne doesn't shove away from the table and throw the damn microscope at the wall. I was tempted a few times in the middle of the night last night.

Daphne moves a few dials on the microscope to get a better view and then shakes her head. "They are so volatile," she whispers. Then she grins up at me. "Our super cells are like Logan cells right now. Hot, angry, wanting to take out the opponent right away."

I puff out my chest. "And what's wrong with that?"

She raises an eyebrow at me. "It doesn't always get the job done. This is going to require patience. And time."

Then her eyes go distant and she starts to tap her teeth with the tip of her nails. A classic Daphne tell that she's having a big idea.

"The current serum is made from the distilled essence

from the *x hybrida rose*, right? From pulped petals and blossoms?"

Her bright green flecked eyes come to mine, lit with excitement. "But what if it's like the yew tree?"

"The what now?"

"Taxol, from the yew tree!"

She zooms backwards and turns so fast with her wheelchair that she almost pulls a wheelie on her way over to a computer in the corner. I can barely keep up with her.

By the time I join her, she's already got several webpages pulled up.

"Oh, *Taxol*." I thought the name sounded familiar, but now that I see what she's pulled up, I'm reminded of exactly where I've seen the name. It's also a non-chemotherapy drug, developed from— "the bark of yew trees," I remember out loud.

"Exactly," Daphne says like I just solved the puzzle.

"What does that have to do with us?"

But Daphne has buzzed to the other side of the room and is pulling out several three-ring binders of old experiments off the shelf. She's skimming through and discarding almost as fast as she can pull them down.

"Daph, what are you looking *for*?"

"I know when we first discovered the oncologic applications for the hybrida essence, Belladonna did studies on the properties of the entire plant. Where are those? Are they only at the Belladonna offices?"

I'm still not sure where she's going but I can help. "I have copies of all of Belladonna's records."

She pauses a moment, her head swinging around my direction.

I hold up my hands in a what? gesture. "It was part of the deal when I bought the patents back. I said I wanted to know what I was buying and I wanted all accompanying research. I have copies of everything."

This time it's her shaking her head. "You conniving little..."

"Do you want to finish that sentence, or do you want help finding what you're looking for?"

Her face stays hard only another moment before she breaks up laughing. "You're incorrigible. But I guess you're my incorrigible. Okay, get your butt over here and help me find what I'm looking for."

I'll accept any excuse to be close to her. I scooted over to her side.

"What is it that we're looking for again?" I ask as I start to sort through the endless shelves of binders. They could have sent the information to me digitally but that would've made it easy on me. Instead, boxes upon boxes of these binders were delivered.

"Ha! Sounds like Dad," Daphne says before going a little sad. But soon she's too busy flipping through binders, her eyes scanning pages, and she's distracted, thank gods.

I grab a couple of binders as well, and am just about to ask again what we are looking for when Daphne suddenly slams down the binder she's looking at and declares, "Ha! There! Look!"

I lean over her shoulder and look. At first all I can see is the page full of running columns of numbers. Gibberish. But then I look at the top and sides of the page and start to decipher what the numbers represent. What it all means.

"Holy..."

"Shit!" Daphne finishes excitedly for me. "Holy shit, right?" she whispers. "We've been using the wrong part of the plant. In the yew tree, the medicine is in its bark. We've been using the rose, but the real medicine is in the *thorns*."

TWELVE

Logan

NO. It can't be that simple. I tell Daphne as much.

But she just pounds her fingers at the numbers on the page. "We weren't trying immunotherapy before. We were just trying to kill the cells. But now that we're trying to insert living cells that reproduce and target the diseased cells, just *look*—"

She slides the notebook in front of me. "The properties of the blossoms and pulp that we thought we might have to try to figure out how to synthesize and allow to fix our longevity problem?" she shakes her head and thumps the binder again. "It's all here already. We were just looking in the wrong place. Or, when we were looking in the right place, we were looking for the wrong thing."

I keep staring down at the numbers. Could it be real, what she's saying? Or is she just desperate and seeing miracles that aren't really there?

Even more dangerous? What she's saying makes sense.

A tremor works its way through my body. And it's only then that I realize, deep down, I've been absolutely sure that I will lose her. That we're living on borrowed time. That something and someone so good and precious could never truly be mine.

For all my brash confidence in declaring I would cure her, I knew in reality the fickle fates would snatch her away far too soon. But I ignored all my fear for her.

She needed strength and optimism so I gave her strength and optimism. And ignored my own underlying terror of what I was sure would come.

But what if that's just my own fucked up past and not... real? What if she doesn't have to die from this? What if I *don't* have to be punished forever for my sins?

I can't speak, can barely breathe as I hurry over and pull on a fresh pair of medical gloves, then get the blood drawing kit out and ready.

Daphne is quiet and wide-eyed as I approach her with the kit. I think the ramifications of what we might have just stumbled on are finally starting to hit her. But at least the blood draw is familiar. I wrap the rubber tubing around the upper top of her arm, find the vein, and draw several tubes of blood.

"Do we need to go harvest some vines and thorns from the greenhouse?" Daphne asks.

"No, I have some on hand already." A good thing, because the process of distilling even a milliliter of concentrated oil from any part of a rose takes a lot of raw material and processing.

Daphne claps. "So we can really see if this will work?"

"The batch might be too old, so we might get inconclusive results, don't get your hopes up—"

"This is going to be great. Stop being such a fart in a jam jar!"

Okay, that made me smile. "I can't remember, is that one Scottish?"

"Welsh."

THIRTEEN

Daphne

"BABE. Babe. Wake up. The results are in."

I roll over and squint at Logan. He doesn't look happy or sad. He just looks like Logan—intense. His intensity softens as he takes in my face.

"What is it?" I whisper around the terror in the pit of my stomach. "Did it work?"

He leans closer and for a horrible moment I just know he's going to say it failed, and hold and comfort me.

But then he says: "It did, baby. It worked."

I gasp as the fist around my middle abruptly lets go. "Oh my god," I sag forward, into Logan's arms. "Oh my god."

There is so much to do, so much I want to ask him, but his mouth is on mine and in this moment I can't do anything but be with him.

I claw off the bed sheets and my clothes, and clamber onto Logan, our lips frantic on each other's. He turns so we're both lying side by side on the bed, still clinging to one another and kissing. I'm breathing him in, deep lungfuls of oxygen and Logan. He is my source.

"I need you," he murmurs against my throat. He's still half-clothed, but my hands are up under his shirt, stroking over his acres of muscles. I scoot into place under him and hiss when he breaches my entrance. I dig my nails into his skin, urging him faster. I want him to ride me hard and let our orgasms blow up like a summer storm, quick as lightning. I want to feel him the next day, and forever.

But he won't let me. He sets the pace, brutally slow, surging into me with increasing force.

Pleasure surges, a white hot force burning through me. I convulse around him, and cry out as his cock continues to batter me.

Orgasms cascade through me, each greater than the last. They hit me from all sides and spin me sideways. The only constant is Logan, rocking over me, grinding against me.

When he finally comes, I hang on for dear life and hope this moment is real.

He collapses over me and I cling to him, not wanting him to shift his weight. He's my rock, pinning me to earth. My knight who fought Death and won. Strange that winning feels as scary as losing.

I speak my worry before it chokes me. "It might not work again. I mean, we'll have to run more tests."

"Already started them." He raises his head, and his certainty blows my doubts away. "But this is it, baby. We found the answer."

And I know it's true.

LOGAN

I look down at the beautiful woman lying in my arms and my mind starts spinning. I can't believe we've found the answer after all these years. Now we just need to synthesize the production of our new drug.

But it's only now as I lay here that I start to think through the actual practicalities of that. I just saw the results, verified them twice to make sure I wasn't getting excited about nothing, then ran up here to Daphne to tell her the good news.

In other plant-based drug trials, especially one based on a limited supply like ours when such a massive amount of product is needed to produce even a milliliter...and Daphne will need a lot more than that...

Now that we know the molecular makeup, we have to create a synthetic form. They did it for Taxol, the cancer drug discovered from the bark of the yew tree Daphne mentioned the other day.

A pit forms in my stomach. But it could take years. Does Daphne have years? But we made the discovery, I could get her in the first clinical trial. As long as we are in control of production.

I glance around us at the cold stone walls.

A makeshift basement lab in a cold, drafty castle is not going to cut it. We need a lab. A fully functioning, fully-staffed lab working around the clock on this.

My chest goes tight as I roll out of bed as smoothly as I can, careful not to wake Daphne. Where the hell am I going to get a lab?

Belladonna has the labs but as the Rose Garden banquet made clear, they're far more concerned with making their new business partner Adam Archer happy than maintaining any relationship with Daphne. And after punching their golden boy plus having security called on me...

Shit! Why couldn't I keep my fucking temper under control?

I storm back down the stairs and head straight for the liquor cabinet. But before I can pour myself two fingers of scotch, I slam the cabinet closed.

I need to be clearheaded. *Think. Think.* I slam my head with my palm.

My mentor left me with this place and a fair chunk of money, but it's not an unending well of resources. I've been sparing no expense as it is, and am running dangerously low on liquid capital. But if Daphne died, what did it matter? What did any of it matter?

Now, though. To get so close and not be able to go the distance...

No. My fists clench.

I'll never give up on her.

I breathe out long and deep.

Today was a success. Daphne has a future now. And I will do anything, pay any price...

Humble myself in any way.

I look up, nodding. I know exactly what I have to do.

I STAND with my arms crossed, glaring up at the tall highrise with Archer Industries emblazoned across the top. And the entrance. And on signs all over the sidewalk.

Seems like a sign of insecurity to me if you feel like you have to plaster your name over everything.

Get it over with. Stop stalling.

My feet stay rooted in place.

There's only one thought that finally gets me moving: *for Daphne.*

I force my arms to my side and push through the revolving doors.

I take it as a great sign when the security guard reaches for his Taser the second I walk in. He's a big bastard, I'll give him that. Tall, with a shaved head, and muscles that strain his uniform, Adam obviously got this guy for actual security and not just some ex-mall-cop looking for an easy pension.

I pause in the doorway, holding my hands up. "I come in peace. I just want to see Mr. Archer. Junior," I clarify. I think Adam's dad still has offices in the building even though he only works part-time now after passing off most responsibilities to Adam the past few years.

"He'll want to take the meeting." I have no doubt that Adam will relish in the opportunity to see me eat crow.

The security guard doesn't move his hand off his Taser. What, do they have me on a watchlist here or something? Or is it just my face that has this guy so damn Taser happy?

I tamp down my temper that rises at the thought. This isn't about me. I'll just have to keep reminding myself of that over and over as I wait as patiently as I'm able while the security guard calls upstairs.

I can't hear what he's saying, since he's stepped behind a partition, but he glances my way often as the conversation goes on for some time before the security guard finally buzzes me through.

He's glaring at me as he hands me a visitor's pass. "Straight to the top floor. Don't make any detours or you'll be escorted from the building immediately."

I grin at him, making sure to turn the mangled left side of my face towards him as I do. "Whatever you say, boss."

He glowers and looks like he's about to yank the pass back, but I'm already halfway toward the elevator banks.

Far too quickly, I'm at Adam's office door. His assistant rushes me right in. Before I'm ready, frankly.

Then I'm standing in front of him. My arch enemy. The man who almost fucking killed me. And I'm here to ask him a favor.

My gut roils but I stand my ground and hold my shoulders straight. "Adam." I incline my head in greeting.

He stands as well, but makes no move to come around from behind his desk. Instead he crosses his arms. "To what do I owe the pleasure?"

"We finally did it. We found a cure. For Battleman's."

Adam doesn't so much as twitch. It's as if I didn't even speak. The bastard is going to make me work for it.

"Daphne's life can be saved now. It doesn't have to be like it was for her mom. Do you get what I'm saying?" I ask when he still doesn't respond.

Finally, he arches an eyebrow. "What's any of this got to do with me?"

Furious fire burns in my gut but I bite it down. Of course he's going to play games. It's the only way he knows. If I'm going to get anywhere with him, I have to play it and outmatch him. All the while letting him think he's winning.

"I own all the patents. But you know that since you've acquired Belladonna. Belladonna doesn't own any of the proprietary research—it's all mine. But I'll sign it all back to you."

He barks out a merciless laugh. "And why would you do that?"

"Because, you idiot, I would do anything, give up anything, to save Daphne's life." I can't help my stoic mask slipping and some of my anger bubbles out.

"Ah, there he is," Adam says, smiling in satisfaction. "There's the snarling beast I'm used to."

"You know what, fuck it," I say. "We hate each other's guts. If we had the opportunity, maybe we'd even kill each other."

He smiles at that and his eyes go disturbingly dark. Oh, this fucker wants to kill me, there's no doubt about that. Truth is, if I could get away with it, or even if I couldn't and there was no Daphne, I just might…

But there *is* Daphne.

"But I'm gambling on the chance that you love money more than you hate me. And there's a shit ton of money in this for you. We need a lab to synthesize the new drug."

"But it won't be applicable just for Battleman's," I hurriedly continue. "What we are developing will be the new face of the fight against cancer. This is a gold mine and you can have all the profits. We just need the lab."

Adam eyes me quizzically, his hand going to his chin. He is quiet a long while before finally asking, "And Daphne will die without this?"

His question shouldn't annoy me but it does. Does he still have feelings for her after all? But again, I swallow my pride. "She *might* be able to survive this latest relapse, but considering her family history…" I close my eyes and nod, finally telling the truth that I haven't even admitted to myself. "Yes, she will eventually die without this. If not this time, then the next."

Adam swears under his breath. At least I'm finally getting through to him.

I look up to find him staring out the window. "So you'll help? We can make a deal? My patents for your laboratories?"

For another long moment, Adam's silent.

When he finally does start to speak, it's not the simple yes I'm expecting.

"Do you know when I first met you, I liked you a lot," he says. "I thought you were 'of the earth.' That was the gracious term my mother used for people like you. The unfortunate poor."

I grind my teeth. *You need him. You can put up with his elitist bullshit meanderings for a few minutes and then you'll be out of here.*

"But then I got to know you. And that's when I realized you didn't know your place. You were too big for your own britches." My fists clench but I stay quiet as he continues. "We could have been a team from the beginning. Unstoppable. Your research skills. My charisma and connections."

He finally turns from the window and looks at me. "But you just wouldn't play ball, would you? It was your arrogance. You just had to have your name on everything. You had to have all the praise and adulation."

Is he fucking serious? This is literally the guy who plasters his name on every single fucking thing he can. He can't blame it on his dad, either. I know it's been him who's pushed to have the Civic Center renamed the Adam Archer Civic Center after donating fifty million to have it renovated.

You need the labs. It's Daphne's life.

So I stay quiet in spite of my seething anger. I knew this wouldn't be easy. But does this asshole have to make it so damn hard?

"Making me look like a fool in front of Dr. Laurel all the time. Even in front of that dumb, scrawny little kid of his." Adam shakes his head and walks over to a cabinet. Why am I not shocked when he opens it to display a hidden liquor cabinet. "But he's gone now."

He pours some expensive looking bourbon and then downs it.

"I tried getting rid of you." He shakes his head. "But they always say the roaches will survive the apocalypse. I guess street rats are the same." He pours himself more bourbon and smiles my direction, holding up the glass in cheers.

"And now, well, if there is a disease that's going to rid the world of that little bitch, Daphne, what can I say?" Adam shrugs his shoulders dramatically. "It's just natural selection at work, man."

I'm going to fucking kill him.

I'm across the room with my hands around his neck before I'm fully aware of what I'm doing. Two seconds later, an alarm is going off and security guards are charging into the room and pulling me off him.

"You're dead!" I shout at him. "If you come near her, I'll—"

But a blow by the huge security guard from downstairs cuts off my words.

Pain explodes across my face, and then the world goes dark.

FOURTEEN

Daphne

I DIDN'T THINK anything of it when Logan said he was going out. He doesn't go out often, but sometimes we need groceries or the like. And he said he'd be right back.

I was a little worried when I didn't hear from him after a few hours. He usually texts or calls if he's running late. So when I finally heard my cell ring, the anxiety I had been feeling finally calms.

Until I saw it was Armand calling, not Logan. Only to pick up the call and find it was Armand calling *about* Logan.

Because Logan was in jail!

I push my wheelchair to maximum speed as Armand holds open the door to the County Sheriff's office.

I race my chair right up to the counter. "I'm here for Logan Wulfe."

Sitting in the chair, I can barely see over the counter to make out the face of the woman attending the front desk.

I start to wobbly climb out of the chair when Armand puts a hand on my shoulder.

"Can she go see my client while I work out the details of his release?"

"You a lawyer?" the woman asks.

Armand leans in and smiles coyly. "Something like that."

The woman, who looks to be in her early fifties, and has a face that reminds me of a bulldog, immediately softens under Armand's charms. "All right, but it's a hell of an expensive bail. Quarter mill."

Armand doesn't flinch. "Money is no object for my client."

The woman's eyes brighten and I want to gag. "Where is Logan? Can I see him now?"

"Marv!" the woman rears back and yells. Even Armand winces at her ear-splitting volume, though he smiles through it.

An older Hispanic man in uniform ambles around the corner. "Take this one back for visiting hours with the new one. With the—" the woman makes a face and gestures at her left cheek. Like she has any room to comment on someone's appearance. Besides, Logan's gorgeous. If this stupid cow can't look past a little scarring to see that, then she's—

"This way, Miss," Marv says, gesturing me to follow behind him.

He leads me to a large room with empty tables that reminds me of a hospital cafeteria. It's empty apart from Marv and me.

But about five minutes later, the door cracks open and then an attendant leads Logan in. His hands are cuffed behind his back and I can't hide the noise of distress that comes from the back of my throat.

I reach for the controls of my wheelchair to go to him, but Marv puts a hand out to stay my action. "No contact," he says kindly. "Otherwise they'll send him back."

I yank my hand back from my controls. I can't stand the thought of getting this close to him and them sending him away again.

"Are you okay?" I call.

His eyes are stormy as he gets closer. "You shouldn't be here. What are you doing out of the house? You aren't strong enough—"

"Don't you dare tell me what I'm strong enough for, Logan Wulfe. Now tell me right this second what's going on. How did you get here? What happened?"

He sinks down heavily in the chair across from me. The attendant undoes the cuffs at his back but warns again about no contact.

When Logan's eyes come to me, they are so full of remorse.

"I'm so sorry," he whispers, sounding broken. "I failed you."

Oh my gosh, he's killing me. "Logan, tell me what's going on, right this second. I'm freaking out."

So he does. He tells me all of it. About how we have to synthesize the drug for it to really be an effective solution for me. About how we needed Belladonna's labs. How we needed Adam.

And how Adam wouldn't help.

How Adam sees this as his final act of revenge...

Me *dying*.

Logan didn't put it that way, but I can finally read between the lines. I can finally see Adam for the monster Logan always said he was.

Logan's no fool. He can see what I've just figured out.

"But we're not going to let that happen," he says adamantly. "We'll find another way. There's always something else we can do. We'll find a way to manufacture enough doses for you, even if we can't synthesize it on a large scale in the beginning, I swear I'll save you—"

I reach for his hand across the table before I remember it's forbidden and pull back.

"Oh Logan. You should've talked to me first."

He just shrugs and I know that if he had to do it over, he wouldn't have changed a thing about what he did if there was even the smallest chance it might've worked. Logan will never see any other way. Like my father, he'll fight this until my dying day.

But unlike a month ago, that doesn't scare me. It doesn't make me want to run away.

For the first time, maybe ever in my whole life, I'm looking the truth in the face.

I might die.

Maybe this year. Maybe next. Maybe I survived this relapse and it comes again for me in three years, or five.

This was always my destiny.

Maybe my problem is that I've been fighting it.

But what if I stop fighting? What if I stop worrying about tomorrow, something I obviously have zero control over?

What if I decide to just live the fuck out of today, come what may?

I look at the man across the table from me, and so much emotion and love wells up in my chest. "Ask me again."

Logan's so dejected, I'm not sure he hears me at first. "What?"

"Ask me again," I whisper, excitement brimming in my voice.

Logan gulps, understanding finally coming into his confused eyes. He doesn't look like he believes what I'm saying, but he's a smart man. "Will you marry—"

"Yes!"

He leaps out of his chair, much to the consternation of the two guards standing at the door. It doesn't stop Logan, though. He comes and throws his arms around me, kissing me hard.

I laugh, tears pouring from my eyes even as I push on his chest, urging him back. "The guards," I laugh through his kisses.

Logan pulls back and holds his hands up right as they are about to grab him. "We just got engaged," he says. "Give a guy a break."

The guard just glares at him. "You know this means you have to get another full cavity search."

Logan just grins at him. "I won't enjoy it too much if you don't."

I laugh out loud and Logan winks at me, the entire atmosphere of the room turned on its head from five minutes ago.

The guards make Logan put his hands on his head before cuffing him again, but he's grinning the whole time.

"Armand's working to get you out on bail," I call.

"Perfect," Logan says over his shoulder, struggling to see me while being dragged away by the guards. "Because I'm marrying your gorgeous ass as soon as physically possible. You can plan it while they do the paperwork."

I laugh again, a gut laugh from deep in my stomach, because I doubt that Logan is kidding or exaggerating at all.

Looks like I'm getting married. S*oon*.

FIFTEEN

Daphne

I STARE at the mirror image of a woman in white. She has a bloom on her cheeks and roses in her hair. Yes, she's in a wheelchair, but she looks healthy, strong. There's a glow about her, along with a restless energy that comes from nervousness. But underneath it all, there's strength.

The woman is me. And today is my wedding day. My real one.

Outside, the staff Armand hired is putting the final touches on the bridal walkway. When I asked for a simple ceremony, Armand gave me a big grin.

"Simple and classic," he promised, and then added, "For the ages."

His statement didn't reassure me at all.

"I'm getting married," I whisper to the woman in the mirror, and her lips curve in a Mona Lisa smile. My hair and make up are done, and I'm in the most gorgeous dress I've ever worn. The frothy skirt is tailored to look good whether I stand or sit in a wheelchair. The beaded bodice hugs my curves.

"Darling! You look fabulous," Armand breezes in and air kisses me as if he's been gone an age instead of a half hour. He personally oversaw my hair and makeup, keeping me smiling with his quips and antics. Then he gave me a moment of quiet, while he checked on everything else.

"Thanks," I grin up at him. "I know an excellent hairdresser."

"Don't you just?" The way he fusses over my hair for another minute tells me he's stalling.

"Armand, it's already perfect." I bat his hand away. "Tell me what's wrong."

"Well... there's good news and bad news."

"Of course there is." I blow out a breath. The fact that this wedding is happening at all defies the gods. As soon as I think it, I shove the thought away and give Armand a little smile. "Bad news first."

"It's raining. Not hard. Just a light rain. We're keeping the guests in the reception tent until it passes—which should be soon. And you know what they say!" Armand holds up a finger and recites. "A wet knot is not easily untied."

I realize I'm fiddling with a bead on my dress's bodice and fold my hands in my lap. "Do they really say that?"

"Oh yes, honey." He raises his hand as if he's being sworn in to testify.

"Okay," I can't help but smile at his sincerity. "And the good news?"

"The good news is we covered the area for the ceremony with a hanging garden, and it's keeping that area mostly dry."

My jaw drifts to the floor. "I'm sorry...did you say 'hanging garden'?"

"Mmmhmmm. I wanted them over the dance floor, but we'd already done the floor. And a garden above and below is just overkill."

"Overkill," I repeat. "What do you mean? What did you do to the floor?"

"Oh, you will *love* it. It's a see through platform—a glass case, actually—and inside is a bed of flowers—roses of course—and ferns. You'll be dancing over a garden all night."

"Oh, wow," is all I can say.

"Yes, *wow*." He kneels and fusses with my hem. "Don't you worry. We're going to get this party started as soon as the rain leaves. Which it should, soon. I have virgins on standby to sacrifice to the gods, in case we need extra insurance to be sure this wedding goes off without a hitch. Anal virgins. It was too hard to find the other kind."

"Haha," I say weakly.

Armand stands and dusts off his hand, straightening his own tux jacket. He looks incredible, but I'm suddenly too nervous to speak. A young man in his own tuxedo ducks in and signals Armand before rushing out again.

"That's our cue." Before I can protest, Armand pushes my wheelchair to the front door.

A sense of readiness cloaks me as I look out onto the lawn. Armand's staff has performed a miracle, transforming Thornhill into a wonderland.

The reception tent is a vast white bird poised in flight. Beside it is a canopied area for the main ceremony covered by a sort of lattice work dripping with wisteria. Guests are making their way to the chairs, escorted by men in tuxes.

"We toweled off the entire ceremony area," Armand tells me.

"It looks perfect." I motion him to push me forward onto the wheelchair ramp so I can see how they decorated the front of the house. There's a green ivy canopy that wasn't there when I rolled in last night.

A stream of men and women in tuxedos and lovely gowns keep coming and muttering reports to Armand.

"All guests seated," one blue-haired woman announces. She gives me a thumbs up before walking off.

"This is it," Armand murmurs as a young man runs up and stands at attention holding a bouquet of peach colored roses. My bouquet. "You ready?"

"Yes," I touch the controls to direct the wheelchair. They built a ramp from the front door all the way to the wedding ceremony area, and sprinkled it with rose petals. My own red carpet.

Armand is still fussing with my hair, arranging each individual curl to his satisfaction. "The rose petals won't be a problem? We can clear the ramp—"

"The rose petals are fine."

"All right, babygirl." One hand swipes at his eyes as he lays the bouquet in my lap. "You look beautiful." He bends and air kisses either cheeks, ever careful to not smear my makeup. "Your mother would be so proud."

"Thank you," I whisper and he steps away, dabbing his own eyes.

My limbs feel weak as I face the long, long ramp to the ceremony area and the waiting guests. Soft symphony music wafts over the lawn.

There's no one to escort me down the aisle, and I like it that way. I live my own life. I come to Logan of my own volition. I will navigate my own way into the life of my dreams.

I roll myself down the newly made ramp. As I get close, a hidden signal warns the musicians to end their song with a long, lingering note. And then a harp starts to pluck a delicate version of The Swan by Saint-Saëns. The heartbreaking melody flows out from under the hanging garden.

For a moment, the notes and the scent of flowers swirl together, like something out of a dream. This moment is so beautiful. So longed for.

The perfection is painful, and for a second I feel as if I'm going to crack in two.

My mother's angel statue is off to the side. The way the sculpture's face is angled, it'll look like she's watching the ceremony.

"Love you, mom," I mouth. And as I roll the final few feet to the first row of chairs, the sun breaks from the clouds, warming my back.

I urge my chair faster. The guests all rise as one, but I can't look to the left or right. I don't realize I'm holding my breath until I see Logan. He stands, a monolith in black. I think he's the only one not wearing a tux. He joked he was going to wear a lab coat, and he did. Armand almost had a heart attack.

There's a sprig of green pinned to his jacket. I focus on it as I get closer. It's a clipping from a bush, an evergreen of some sort, frozen in resin. Needles and a single red berry.

"Yew," I whisper to myself, and am rewarded by my fiancé's smile.

I reach the end of the aisle. The priestess motions for the audience to be seated. The harpist ends one song and starts another.

I take a moment to view the guests. There's Armand, just settling into his seat. He was probably rearranging the final floral flourish himself.

Beside him, Cora Ubeli glows in a sky blue dress. Her two children sit straight and solemn between her and her husband. I give Cora a little wave and she beams at me. Her adorable young daughter tugs her mom's sleeve and points at me, and Cora leans down to whisper in the little girl's ear. Both mother and daughter have bright blue eyes.

I could have planned on rising out of my wheelchair for the ceremony—I am strong enough—but today is going to be long and I want to conserve my strength. I hesitate with my hands on the armrests, wavering on the decision. Sit or stand?

Logan makes it for me. Gracefully for a man of his size, he lowers himself to one knee. The look of love in his blue eyes washes over me, and I have to turn away. Judging from a few sniffles in the audience, I'm not the only one blinking away tears.

"Daphne," he murmurs. "Look at me."

"I can't," I whisper, blinking rapidly. "You're gonna make me cry." I half laugh and breathe deep, trying to push my tears back.

"It's okay, baby." His big hand hovers at my cheek, dabbing my made-up face with a white handkerchief. "I've got you."

"So I look all right?" I can face him now. The tightness in my chest has eased, washed away as his scent surrounds me. There's just Logan and me here. Nothing else matters.

"You look beautiful." His deep voice is balm to my soul.

"Thank you." I keep my eyes down, fastening onto the sight of our hands entwined. The ceremony proceeds. Most of it's a blur, but a few moments I'll remember forever.

The breeze stirring the flowers overhead.

The slanting sunlight illuminating my mother's statue, haloing her peaceful mien.

The way Logan's voice stumbles on the words "in sickness and in health."

The way his hands squeeze mine. He doesn't let go—even to slide on the ring. It was as if he expected me to disappear mid-ceremony.

"In sickness and in health," I repeat, covering his big hand with mine. "'Til death...and beyond." It's my turn to grip him hard.

I'm never letting you go. Death be damned.

I barely hear the priestess's final words. Logan is smiling at me. He leans in and brushes his lips over mine.

I blink at him, suddenly dizzy. "We did it?"

"We did it. Come here," his arms are around me, pressing me closer as he gives me a deeper kiss. He scoops me up, his lips never leaving mine as the crowd rises to their feet and roars their approval.

Logan carries me through a shower of rose petals—shot from a cannon manned by Armand himself. We end up in the reception tent where there's a huge white throne for me to sit on to receive guests. The Ubelis are first in line.

"I feel like a queen," I whisper to Cora Ubeli.

"Queen for a day. You look beautiful." She bends and kisses my cheek. "Congratulations."

The next few hours are a blur. I greet guests and shake hands until I feel like my hand is going to fall off.

Then a five course dinner—which I can barely eat because every other second people clink their glasses and Logan and I have to kiss. Not that I mind.

After the last course, before the cake cutting, a band called The Muses strikes up their top hits. And I have enough energy to rise and walk on my own to the elevated dance floor—which is a glass case filled with a carpet of ferns and roses, exactly as Armand described.

I squeal as Logan lifts me into the air and whirls me around. But he doesn't let me back down to the ground. He keeps me in his arms as we sway to the music.

"I'm walking better now," I whisper in his ear, my arms around his neck. "You don't have to carry me everywhere."

He just nuzzles his face into the crook of my neck. "Now that you're Mrs. Logan Wulfe, you're nuts if you think I'm ever letting you go, even for a single damn minute."

I don't expect the absolute explosion of joy in my chest, and not expecting it makes it all the sharper. This was never supposed to be my life. I'm not the girl who gets the fairy-tale ending.

But being surrounded by our friends and loved ones, at the wedding straight out of my dreams, being held by a man who loves me with his whole heart, what else can you call it?

Does he feel it? Does Logan feel the perfection he's given me? That I was cracked and broken before he found me, but he was the only medicine I ever needed. The balm to my broken heart after I lost my mother and my father's rejection.

And, feeling all his heart muscles beneath my soft body, I know he's so much more than that. He's the igniter of passions, the storm that shook up my staid, colorless world, and he's been my hope and strength at times these past few months when I couldn't manage any on my own.

He's the love of my life. My partner on this journey. The other half of my soul.

I tip my head back to look at him and see everything I'm feeling reflected in his dark eyes.

I can't help drawing his head down to mine. He's still careful, but I've been more desperately physical lately than ever. I think both of us need it. To prove to ourselves that we are real and still here together.

And when his lips touch mine—

Heaven.

There's a tent full of people watching us but that doesn't stop Logan. He teases at the seam of my lips with his tongue and when I open to him, I only barely manage to stifle my moan, even though we're in the middle of the dance floor. But I've never been able to manage restraint when it comes to Logan.

He's just started to deepen the kiss when there's a shrill whistle. Like someone blowing on an actual whistle. What on earth—?

I pull back from Logan lips in confusion. Is this some kind of gag before Armand gives his toast?

Whatever I expect to see, it's not a brigade of serious-faced policemen, along with some men in scrubs behind them, barging into the wedding. It's not hard to see where they're headed.

Straight for Logan and me.

"What's the meaning of this?" Armand demands, trying to step in front of the most senior-looking policeman.

"Are you the groom?" the hard-faced policeman asks.

Armand's face registers confusion but he doesn't answer. Apparently he doesn't need to.

Because rounding the corner is Adam Archer.

"No," Adam stands arrogantly and points to Logan. "That's him. That's the man you're here to arrest."

SIXTEEN

Daphne

"WHAT?" I screech just as Logan finally drops me to the ground and steps in front of me, shielding me from Adam.

"What's this about, Archer? You here to finally have it out with me like a man?" Logan sneers, looking around at the huge posse Adam brought with him. "Or like always, are you getting others to do your bullying for you. Can't damage that manicure, can you?"

Adam's face goes red and the hand he has pointed at Logan starts to shake a little, but he just repeats, "There he is. Arrest him."

"On what grounds?" Armand demands, trying to get in front of the policeman again.

"We have a warrant for his arrest," Adam crows.

"On. What. Grounds?" Armand repeats, looking like he's barely keeping his temper, even though during every interaction I've ever had with him, he seemed like the most even-tempered man, almost lackadaisical in his approach to serious life.

"On the grounds that he's a dangerous psycho," Adam says. "He's attacked me and is a mentally unstable public threat. He walks around in a serial killer mask, for gods' sake. He's already violated one restraining order and I have multiple witnesses who heard him threaten my life. The fact that he's gone this long unpunished only highlights the corruption in the underbelly of this city."

The way he's going on, it's like he's trying out a run for mayor. But he's not nearly finished. "So it is the opinion of the great city of New Olympus that he be remanded into the custody of the state for a period of observation for criminal psychosis."

And that's when the camera flashes start to go off.

Son of a— He brought the media, because of course he did.

I should have known he was grandstanding for an audience. And certainly not for our wedding party, all of whom obviously side with us. No, he's speechifying for a much bigger crowd. Maybe even using this as his launching point for a political bid, going on about corruption at a wedding where the Ubelis are present, when everyone knows that they are the King and Queen of all Underworld activity on the East Coast.

Destroying Logan's reputation in the meantime by using him as a scapegoat? Now I know this is classic Adam. This is how he works. Who he is.

I feel Logan tense in front of me and my arm shoots out to restrain him. "He's baiting you," I hiss. "If you beat his face in like *you* want, you'll just be giving him everything *he* wants. Please, babe."

I intertwine my fingers with his. "Not today. We won't give him what he wants today."

Logan swallows hard, really hard, but he gives me an almost imperceptible nod.

And he manages it, too.

The policeman and medical staff get to us and begin reaching for Logan.

"I'll come quietly," Logan says, keeping his voice measured and calm. "There's no need for a scene."

But it's as if he didn't even say a word. I'm just about to let go of his hand when I'm suddenly grabbed by my left arm and yanked sharply away. My arm is wrenched in such a way that I can't help crying out in pain.

And that, apparently, is Logan's breaking point.

His head snaps my direction. "Leave her be."

But the asshole cop, who I now realize must be working in cahoots with Adam, just chuckles in Logan's face and then spits at his feet, at the perfect angle so the cameras can't catch it.

"Boy, where you're going, you ain't gonna have no say about what happens to Little Miss here back home. Cuff 'im, men."

Two other men approach with cuffs and that's when all hell breaks loose.

Logan lets out a roar and, standing almost a foot taller than all the other men around him, he starts to fight. At least that's what it looks like from outside the circle that starts to grow around him.

"Logan!" I scream, but I don't know if he can hear anything above the uproar.

Men in uniform start to fly backwards but almost immediately another takes their place.

I start forward but I'm grabbed on both sides. "Let me

go," I shout but Armand at my left and Cora at my right refuse to let me go. And then it's the Ubeli's men in black dragging me backwards away from the fray.

"Logan wouldn't want you anywhere near that," Armand shouts in my ear and that's the only thing that makes me back away. Which unfortunately only gives me a better view of what's happening to Logan because we head a little ways up the hill and now I can see down on the unfolding tableau.

There must be twenty men surrounding Logan and he's swinging and brawling like an enraged animal. He's past reason. That man threatened me and I know, I *know* that all Logan could see in that moment was that he wouldn't be able to protect me if they succeeded in taking him away from my side.

"Stop it, please you have to stop them!" I cry, slumping to my knees, my beautiful wedding dress all but ruined by the wet grass outside the tarped area.

But I can only look on in horror as the cops finally get Logan face down on the ground. Only barely, by the looks of it, and it's taking several men to restrain him there. And then one of the men in scrubs approaches, something in his hand I can't make out.

Until he raises it to Logan's neck and with a sickening realization, I realize exactly what it is.

A syringe.

He presses it to Logan's neck and within thirty seconds, my big, beautiful, virile brand new husband is passed out, sedated like a large, dangerous animal on the floor. Of his own wedding.

And the news cameras were rolling the whole time, capturing the entire thing.

SEVENTEEN

Daphne

LOGAN HAD NO CHANCE. Not with the video from the wedding. Not just on all the news stations playing 24/7, but also all over the internet.

It would have gone better for Logan if he wasn't so damn strong. But he just kept knocking them down. Even I haven't been able to avoid the videos. I was there and they make it look so much more dramatic, maybe because of the filters and the cinematic music always layered on top—

And the fact that an ambulance had to be called for four of the policeman didn't help his case—even though I know for a fact that none of those supposed 'terrible injuries' actually lead to anyone needing to be taken to the hospital and that it was likely all just more fanfare and showcasing by Adam to win points in the press.

"It's a mess," I confess to Armand, face in my hands.

"It's bullshit is what it is." Armand stands and paces back and forth in my beautifully restored Thornhill living room. Every day I'm living in the reminder of Logan's love and every day it pierces all the deeper that he's not here with me to enjoy it.

We should be on our honeymoon right now, and instead, he's locked away in some cold, padded cell at Maniae Hospital for the Criminally Insane.

Just, what the fuck, world? Why can't we get a damn break? Incurable cancer wasn't enough? Separating us for almost a decade? Fighting past misunderstandings and insecurities and finally finding our way to each other, having the wedding of our dreams only for it to be stolen away before we even get to our *wedding night*?

I officially give up on fairness in the universe.

Armand is feeling less despair and more righteous indignation.

"Cora wants to get involved. She and Marcus have wanted to clean up that corrupt police force for years."

I just gape at him.

"Oh darling, haven't you realized that the Ubelis are the real power in this city? Metropolis, too."

I look around uncertainly, not wanting to gossip about my friends. "But aren't they sort of...I mean I've heard rumors that... Aren't they sometimes involved in some criminal things... Occasionally, I mean?"

Armand laughs out loud, a full-bodied chuckle. It goes on for several minutes and he's wiping his eyes by the end.

"Cora would die laughing if she heard that description of their businesses."

"Oh please don't tell her. I'm sorry, I didn't mean to malign—"

But Armand just sits beside me on the couch and puts an arm around my shoulders, giving me a squeeze. "I'll let you in on a family secret. I think you've earned it. Cora and

Marcus *are* the criminal underworld, darling. And they aren't ashamed of it. They're on the side of the people. On the side of good," he says earnestly in the way only a true friend can.

"They know that if they are running it, the whole world is a lot safer than if the truly evil fucks had their hands on the pulse."

Finally, his jovial expression collapses. "Like those dick-faced cunts at the Metro police that Archer has bought out. Nobody likes a sellout, least of all the Ubelis."

He talks about them like they're all-powerful. "So can they help Logan?"

His lips tighten into a hard line. "Archer's not a complete idiot. He knows aligning himself against you and Logan means making an enemy of them. But there's plenty in this city who think it's time the reign of the Ubelis came to an end and are willing to back him. With his money and his name and frankly his boy-next-door good looks—"

I slam my hands down on the coffee table in front of the couch. "That's such bullshit! He's a monster on the inside and Logan is so wonderf—"

Armand takes my hands in his and looks at me gently, his eyes full of compassion. "I know. I know. We'll find a way out for him. This isn't the end. I promise. All I'm trying to say is you have friends in high places. And we'll do everything in our power to help."

But all I hear is what he isn't saying. He isn't saying he has a direct way to help. He isn't saying they can get Logan out now. All he has are wishes and half-promises. And I appreciate where he's coming from, I really do. Everyone wants to help.

But it doesn't mean they *can*.

I stand on wobbly legs. "Thanks for coming by, Armand. It really means a lot."

Armand stands and hugs me, but as he does, his hands pat down my back, especially around my shoulder blades. "Are you getting enough to eat? Taking care of yourself?"

He pulls back and holds me by my shoulders, inspecting my face even as I roll my eyes.

"I'm fine, I swear." It's mostly true. I'm mostly remembering to eat.

Armand gives my shoulders a slight squeeze. "You have to stay strong for him. Otherwise he'll go crazy. The only thing keeping him sane is knowing that we're out here looking out for you."

I roll my eyes again, because that's so Logan. Worrying about *me* when *he's* the one stuck in an insane asylum.

I walk him to the front door. "How about this? I promise to go eat the biggest lunch possible, and you promise to keep working every connection you have to get Logan out. Deal?"

Armand watches me with that all-too-assessing gaze for another half a minute, then he nods. "Deal."

I wave at him from the doorway before deciding to make good on my promise and head for the kitchen.

I'm opening the refrigerator door to see if anything is left inside or if I need to order more groceries, when a movement catches my eye in my periphery.

I yelp and slam the refrigerator shut when I realize that the movement is a *person*.

A stranger. In my house. In my kitchen. With me. While I am alone.

"Who are you?" I shout even as I reach in my pocket for my phone. Where the hell is my phone? Were they here the whole time Armand was? Why didn't the security alarm go off if they broke in?

The person is short and their back is to me. They're wearing a hoodie and I can't even tell if it's a man or woman, or maybe a teenager, they're so slight. Maybe 110 pounds soaking wet.

Not that I'm taking any chances. I start backing away, my hand scrambling on the counter for anything to protect myself. Naturally, the block of knives is on the opposite counter, closer to my intruder.

My hands close around a rolling pin just as the stranger turns my way.

My fingers lose their grasp and the rolling pin topples to the ground with a loud clatter as I whisper, "Rachel?"

EIGHTEEN

Logan

I'M EARLY to the lab today and haven't had enough caffeine yet. Without thinking, I scrub a hand down my face, then jerk back when I accidentally touch my cheek where Adam decked me last night.

I still can't believe that Dr. Laurel didn't listen to me when I went to his office afterwards to tell him about Adam's schemes. Then again, he's grief stricken. Maybe if I try again today, when he's in a better frame of mind...

I go to the wall and unlatch the sterile equipment cabinet, pulling out the goggles with my name on them. We all started labeling our equipment after some pieces started going missing last year. Now we sign everything in and out.

I ran a group of experiments overnight and I'm eager to look at the slides. So I tug the goggles into position and start on my work, bent over my microscope.

Everything's normal at first. Business as usual.

Until it's not.

It starts as an itch.

And then becomes an uncomfortable tingling.

I ignore it. I have work to do. And I'm hoping Daphne will come in at lunch. If I finish up all the slides, then maybe I can sneak her out of here and we can go to Giuseppe's for pizza and—

The tingling becomes a burning and I push my rolling chair back from the microscope, yanking off my goggles and blinking hard.

What the hell?

I lift my hand to my face but stop just before making contact. Instead, I hurry to the bathroom, shouldering past someone on their way out.

"Hey man, watch out!"

I ignore him and make my way to the mirror, shoving my face towards the glass. It doesn't look that bad. There was only the smallest incision from where Adams class ring caught my cheek last night when he punched me, but now the whole area is puffy and red.

But then, as I watch, red vein-like spindles begin to spider outwards. Down my cheek. Up towards my left eye.

I stumble back from the mirror, grunting in shocked surprise.

But it's not stopping.

It only accelerates as I watch.

I reach my phone to call 911 but by the time I've dialed, the mirror is already revealing a monster.

The infection or whatever it is, is spreading like spilled ink through the veins of my face. And I'm being lit on fire from within. Hellfire. Burning me alive from the inside out.

I vaguely hear the 911 operator over the phone I dropped to the floor but I'm too busy screaming to answer. Without thinking, I raise my hands to my face but as soon as I make contact, the infection spreads to my fingers.

I burst out of the bathroom looking for somebody, anybody to help. But the first person to see me, Sandra from research and development, screams and drops the files she's holding.

"Help," I try to say, but my throat is burning.

I collapse to my knees and that's when I realize I'm dying.

A slow clap comes from the corner. I lift my face, that now feels like an inferno, just in time to make out Adam's satisfied smirk as he stands and claps, as if me dying in front of him is some sort of performance art.

I lunge for him but someone else catches me in their arms.

"Logan!" Daphne tries to catch me, but I'm too heavy, and we both topple to the ground.

No! The only possible thing that could have made this worse is having her witness it. But I'm wrong, so wrong. There is something worse.

Because when I finally managed to pull myself off of Daphne, I see her looking at her own hands in confusion. Seconds before they too begin to redden and then start to disintegrate before my very eyes.

Her ear splitting scream of terror and confusion is the last thing I hear before—

My eyes shoot open and I bolt upright. Or at least I try to.

I barely make it an inch before the restraints strapped around my body on all sides keep me in place.

Because I'm strapped down to a fucking hospital bed. And this isn't a kinky game of power exchange with my Daphne.

I don't know where I am but I know I don't want to be here.

Especially when the door opens and an orderly pops his head in. Then I hear a whispered exchange.

"It's your turn. I don't want to have to deal with that crazy fucker again today. Did you see what they're giving him in his drug cocktail? They should be sedating him but instead they are giving him—" he mentions some drug I'm not familiar with. I guess the other nurse isn't either, because then he clarifies, "It's basically LSD. I don't know what the hell they're thinking. That shit's just going to wind him up and make him twice as crazy while he's all strapped up like that."

"But we get hazard pay and a half," says another male voice. "And I got bills to pay."

"Yeah, I guess," the other guy mutters, though he doesn't sound happy about it. "Don't know what good that's going to do me if I got a broken neck. You see Nick? That guy's a giant, right? But even *Nick* got two of his teeth knocked out bringing this guy in."

My own teeth grate as I strain against the restraints, looking for any weakness I might exploit. But there's so many damn straps up and down my arms and legs, even if I got one free, how the hell am I going to get out of the rest?

Because I have to get back to Daphne. Fuck. *Daphne*. She can't handle this kind of stress right now. It's literally one of the worst things for someone in her condition. How long have I been here? How long since the...the wedding?

My hands fist. I am going to fucking kill Adam Archer for ruining that moment for Daphne. The memory of him clapping while I disintegrate from flesh-eating bacteria in front of him... Bile burns up my throat.

Of course, that's not exactly how that day went down. I

went to the bathroom, saw the redness and swelling, and a couple hours later when the stinging continued, I went to the doctor. And after some tests came back, was immediately admitted to the ICU.

I could never prove it, but I don't doubt it was Adam who ordered the infectious sample from the CDC. Adam who put it on my goggles. Adam who tried to murder me in one of the most horrific ways possible.

And now I'm here for the exact same reason. Adam fucking Archer, taking another swing at me.

As my fury builds, my vision begins to blur. There's a high, slim horizontal window at the top of the wall, and the light begins to shimmer and twist. I blink hard, but the light still dances. I glance around and for the first time notice that the walls aren't that steady either. Everything is swaying slightly.

Fuck, what drugs are they shoving into me without my consent?

Which is when I look down my body and notice the IV stuck in my arm. Shit, they're still actively pumping poison into me.

Get it out. Get it the hell out!

As I watch, the line of the IV starts to undulate like a snake, burrowing into my skin. I twist and scratch, but I'm bound too tightly. I can't get to it to yank it out.

"Help!" I scream as the poison spreads. "Get it out!"

But no one comes. No one ever comes to help.

And then there are a thousand snakes, all skittering through my veins, poison, poison. They'll burn me. They'll chew on me and burn me, eating me alive from the inside out.

I scream and scream, until my voice is hoarse, until I have no more voice, but no one ever comes to save me.

NINETEEN

Daphne

RACHEL SHOVES down the hoodie of her sweatshirt and holds up her hands. "It's me."

Like that's supposed to make me feel better about the situation.

Her normally perfectly styled blonde hair is loose around her face, with dark roots showing. She's in yoga pants and a baggy, shapeless sweater. There are dark craters under her eyes. She looks fragile, but all the more beautiful for it.

Of course she's the one woman who looks amazing even when she's a wreck. I brush crumbs off my lap from the teacakes with Armand, and tug up the sleeve of my boat neck sweater, which has fallen off my shoulder. I look like seven types of shit.

"Daphne, I am so, so, so sorry." She's stopped a few feet away from me, wringing her hands.

I scoff. Does she really expect me to believe that? Especially after she just broke into my house, on top of everything else?

"Adam blackmailed me," she blurts. "I didn't want to help him with any of it."

"What?"

"He's had dirt on me a long time. I know you're mad, and you have a right to be. But I can explain." Her eyes drop to the floor in shame. "A few years ago, remember when my dad needed surgery?"

In spite of myself, my heart tugs. "Rachel, I told you I could help you out, no strings attached."

When she looks up, a tear is streaking down her cheek. "I was too proud. I thought I could fix it on my own."

"How?"

She swipes angrily at her tears and swallows hard.

"Belladonna has an annual slush fund for company parties. It's stupid and nonessential and no one ever usually checks the balance but me since I'm the chair of the committee. I just needed $2000 to pay off the hospital so they wouldn't foreclose on Dad's house. I knew I could pay it back as soon as I got my tax refund. And I did. In full. The money was only missing a few weeks. It seemed harmless."

My thoughts are on a merry-go-round. I was barely able to sleep last night after they took Logan away, but that reminds me—

"You drugged me." The betrayal still cuts deep.

"Not me. *Adam.*" Her voice is desperate. "Look, I know you won't believe me. I can only imagine what he's told you—"

"That you instigated the whole thing so you could sell my pictures to the Inquirer."

"What?" she rage screeches. I flinch. "Sorry," she drops

her voice, still fuming. "I can't believe he accused me. That lying...cheating..."

"Douche canoe?"

"The douchiest!" She throws her hands up in the air. I shouldn't laugh, but it's amazing seeing Rachel like this. Her hair's mussed and her cheeks are red with rage. It's a good look for her.

I want to throw my arms around her. I miss my best friend so badly. But my naïveté has cost me too much, too many times.

So I hold myself back and gesture at the kitchen table. I sit at the opposite side and fold my hands together. "So what happened then?"

She nods, swallowing hard again, and returns to her story. "It should have been harmless. But somebody did notice the money was missing."

"Adam," I say.

Furtively, she looks my way and nods.

"Adam," she agrees. "I didn't even know Archer Industries had access to our books until he showed up in my office one day looking for answers. We weren't officially affiliated with them back then."

I know the answer to that. Dad. No doubt Adam made the request, framing it in such a way as if he was looking out for my dad's interests... When all along it was just another lever of control for Adam, always on the hunt for any weakness.

And he found one in Rachel.

Rachel's eyes are back on the table. "At first it wasn't anything big. He just said I might owe him a favor in the future. Then sometimes he'd show up at my apartment in the middle of the night and I got the idea it was in my best interests not to say no." The last part comes out as a whisper.

"Back then I was still trying to pretend that I was into it. He was hot and New Olympus' Most Eligible Bachelor three years running..."

She sucks in a deep breath. "But then he started dating you." Her eyes dart up to meet mine and then away again. "He said I should encourage it. When I balked, that's when he started to hold the missing money over me. And it only got worse from there."

Her hands shoot across the table and grasp mine. I jump in surprise but she doesn't let go. "But I swear, I never drugged you. I didn't know, that night at his apartment. I swear I didn't know what he was doing. And I didn't let him touch you. I swear, Daphne. You have to believe me. I distracted him the whole night. He was determined to take those damn pictures, but he didn't touch you."

Her impassioned plea and the tears shining in her eyes — Either she's the best damn actress I've ever witnessed in my life or...

I shove out of my chair and move as quickly as my tired body can take me, then I throw my arms around my best friend.

She hugs me back just as fiercely. "I'm sorry. I'm so sorry," she repeats over and over, eventually shaking and sobbing in my arms.

"It's okay," I find myself laughing and soothing her, patting her back. "We were both taken advantage of by The Douchiest Douche."

But when she pulls back, she's shaking her head. "He's more than that. He's evil. And I didn't just come here to apologize."

That's when she starts to pull folders out of a backpack

I didn't even notice she'd brought in. "I came here so that we could take that bastard down. I'm not the only one he's tried to blackmail. And I've got proof."

WITH ARMAND and Cora's help, it takes about four hours to put together the press conference.

Armand himself came to style Rachel and get her camera ready. She's shaking while several news teams set up the lighting and cameras.

"You look perfect," I say. I grab her forearms. "You look fierce. Confident. You can do this."

But she's shaking her head rapidly back and forth. "No, I can't. I'm not like you. I'm not strong."

I barely keep in my laughter. Is she serious? Me, strong? Then again, maybe she's right. Maybe strength is what it's taken all these years to survive. And lately I've been determined not only to survive, but thrive.

So maybe Rachel's right, that does take strength. Incredible strength. And it's okay if it took me a while to get here. Just like it's okay that Rachel's finally discovering that well within herself now.

I move my hands to hers and squeeze hard. "You've got this. I know you do. You're a total badass and now you're going to go show the world that you won't let anybody walk all over you. Because you deserve so much better."

She grins wide at me. "Fucking love you."

She hugs me hard, then pivots and walks out to the podium before I can even return the sentiment.

Lights blaze and cameras flash as she reaches the podium and arranges her notes. Finally, she takes a drink of water from the glass that's been set there and then begins.

"Good evening, ladies and gentlemen. Thank you for coming here tonight. My name is Rachel Simpson and three years ago, Adam Archer began blackmailing me in exchange for sex, corporate secrets, and more recently, in exchange for my cooperation in seducing, then later drugging and taking illegal photographs of his ex-fiancée Daphne Laurel."

There are audible gasps across the room but Rachel isn't nearly done. "Furthermore, while in his acquaintance, I came across evidence that I was only one of many that Adam Archer was blackmailing. Other victims include—"

And then I watch on from the sidelines like a proud mom as she goes on to list a long number of names, both public and private figures. Many of the names of public figures raise eyebrows, including that of New Olympus' chief of police.

The camera lights continue blazing, but half the reporters in the room are scribbling notes while others are on the phone, some even leaving the room to make calls.

And I sit back and smile in satisfaction, knowing that finally Adam Archer's life is about to be blown apart—an experience he's inflicted on so many others.

Karma is sweet.

TWENTY

Logan

THE CREAK of an opening door rouses me from my foggy state. My eyes snap open. I've been lying here for I don't know how long. Long enough for the light in the window to fade. Long enough for the dark to cover me. Long enough to sense when I'm no longer alone.

"Who's there?" My throat is screaming for water.

"A friend." A shadow detaches itself from the wall and drifts to the foot of my bed where it solidifies into the shape of a man. Tall and slender, clad in a tailored grey suit. "Relax. I'm here to rescue you."

Head bowed, he studies my restraints a moment, before reaching in his breast pocket and drawing out a Swiss Army knife. A few short moments and I'm free. My joints creak but I rip out the IV from my arm.

'Thanks' is on the tip of my tongue, but I have no idea what's going on. As far as I know, this man could still be an enemy. A trap.

"Who are you?" I have to squint into the shadows, where he's retreated.

"My name is Sebastian St. James." His cultured voice, smooth and deep, winds its way into my ears. He half smiles as he returns to my side and offers me a bottle of water.

"Never heard of you." But I take the water and gulp it down.

"I've taken great care to remain anonymous. I prefer it."

"Then what are you doing here?"

"I own this building."

"Then you're not a friend." I drop the water bottle on the floor, wishing my strength was back. If I stand now, I don't trust myself to remain upright. If I did, I'd wipe the floor with him.

"I assure you, Dr. Wulfe, I am a friend." He doesn't back away from my glare, but steeples his fingers. "Allow me to start from the beginning. I own a great many things. An empire, built over many years."

"You don't look that old to me," I grunt. The man facing me with such a lack of fear is smooth-faced. Thirty at the most. Young to bear such an air of gravitas.

"I started young. And I have many friends. It's easy to amass the things you want when you're willing to ally yourself with anyone who can help you get them."

"You made a deal with the devil."

"Some say that. Some say I am the devil." His voice holds a note of amusement. "But that has nothing to do with the circumstances right now. Lately I've been interested in expanding my interests into the pharmaceutical realm. I acquired research by a brilliant young doctor, a prodigy of the late Dr. Laurel."

I shake my head. I know where this is going.

"For a while now, I've been investigating Adam Archer. We even signed a temporary agreement for him to use my warehouse as a private research facility."

He spreads his hands to indicate our surroundings. "My own company provides security. Not only to secure the outside of the building, but to monitor the inner workings as well. Imagine my surprise when my secret cameras show a man being held against his will. And not just any man. A former friend, college roommate, and rival of Adam Archer."

He leans in. "And, if my research is correct, the real prodigy of Dr. Laurel. The one Adam Archer would do anything to destroy."

"All right," I say drily. If I wasn't still feeling weak and woozy, I'd be outta here. Since I need a moment to collect my strength, I'm okay with listening to this stranger's soliloquy. "You figured it all out. Now what?"

"We seem to have a common enemy. And common goals. I wish to expand my holdings into the pharmaceutical arena. You want the means and ability to continue your research—starting with the cure for Battleman's. You have the knowledge, I have the labs. If we partner together, we could be behind the medical breakthroughs of this century."

He lowers his hands, his face taking on a wry expression, as if he's amused by his own forthrightness. In the middle of his earnest speech, he looked much younger. "But that comes later. Let us address the matter at hand. Revenge."

"Yes," I growl, unable to stop myself from showing my hand. St. James' expression is perfectly blank. But I understand how he could be as powerful as he claims. If he's able to speak to the heart of the matter, and offer a man exactly what he wants...he could easily rule an empire.

"Anything," I say, even though I suspect I'll regret it. "I'll give you anything to get me out of here and help me bring Adam down."

"Oh, haven't you seen?" He turns away to pick up something—a remote—and points it at the wall. A screen comes down from the ceiling. St. James presses a few buttons and the TV flares to life.

"—following accusations of their former CEO's corporate espionage, insider trading, and sexual assault, Archer Industries stock falls by over thirty percent—"

I watch opened-mouth as Adam Archer is led down a street lined with reporters. Adam himself is flanked by two police officers. His hands are cuffed behind his back.

"What happened?"

"A group of women stepped forward and brought Adam Archer's sins to light. He's been removed as CEO, of course, but it seems he's run from the many charges filed against him. The police are looking for him."

St. James is studying my face but I can't tear my gaze from the screen. The reporter is talking over images of the press conference that broke the news of Adam's deceit. A vaguely familiar blonde woman is speaking. The camera pans and—yes, there's Daphne in her wheelchair, watching. My brave girl.

"Quite a woman," St. James murmurs.

I snap my attention from the screen.

He raises his hands. "No need to glare. I understand she's now your wife."

"Do they really call you the devil?"

"Yes," he says simply. "Mostly in New Rome, my city. Not here. In New Olympus there are other, older powers."

"But you can help me."
"Oh yes." And he smiles.
"Well, then. Let's make a deal."

TWENTY-ONE

Daphne

MY MOTHER IS beautiful as she walks beside me. Long flowing hair, healthy and shining in the bright summer sunshine.

She reaches out and takes my hand. "It's so good to see you. I've missed you so much."

I stop her in front of the garden, roses blooming all around us. "Mama," I cry, a rush of emotion hitting me, I don't even know why. For some reason it feels like I haven't seen her in a long time.

I pull her into a hug, squeezing her close.

"What's got into you?" she asks, chuckling. She rubs my back anyway, just like she used to do when I was sick as a kid.

"I've missed you, too," I say, tears bursting out of my eyes and running down my cheeks, even though I'm not certain where she's been or why we've been separated, or why it's so good to see her right now. To feel her solid in my arms.

She pulls back from me and cups my face, swiping some stray hairs behind my ear. "You listen to me, Daphne Laurel, you are strong and beautiful and you can do anything in this life you set your mind to."

I nod, tears still streaking my cheeks. I hear what she's saying and for the first time, deep in my bones, I believe it.

Just then, the sun starts to set and Mom looks over her shoulder. Then she smiles gently back at me. "It's almost time for me to go."

"No." I shake my head and clutch onto her forearms. "I'm not ready. Just a little longer."

But her smile only gentles further as she pulls away from me. "My wonderful girl," she whispers, giving my hand one last squeeze. "I always wished a love like no other for you, and that you'd live a beautiful life. With someone who could match your beautiful soul."

She beams at me. "I couldn't have left you and been at peace knowing you'd be all alone in the world. But now I can."

"Mama," I call, reaching for her as she backs away, but no matter what I do, she begins to vanish into sudden twilight, while I'm frozen in place.

But it's not scary or sad. It's like what she said. She's leaving now because she's at peace and...

It comes back to me like a whisper on the wind—*it's not your time yet*. And I feel it in my bones. It's not my time now. Maybe not for a long while yet. Maybe not for a whole lifetime.

"Wake up, sleeping beauty."

I jerk awake with a start. To Logan hovering above me on the bed.

I screech and throw my arms around him. "How? How did you get out?"

I wrap my legs around him too, for good measure. "Armand said he'd talk to Marcus but I didn't think they could work this fast—"

"It wasn't Marcus or Armand. It's a long story and I'll tell you later. What's important is," his eyes are shining as he drags me up to a sitting position. "We got a lab. We can mass produce the Battleman's serum."

I blink as he explicitly spells it out for me. "Daph, we have the cure. You'll be cured. Not just of this latest relapse, but completely. We found the cure and we can manufacture it."

It's not your time yet.

Holy shit, Mom knew.

Wait, that's ridiculous, it was just a dream.

But it felt *so* real.

"Why aren't you celebrating?" Logan's exuberance immediately turns to concern. "You should be celebrating. Are you not feeling okay today? Did something happen while I was away? Fuck, have you not been keeping up with the recovery protocols? Dammit, Daph, you promised you wouldn't slip no matter what happened to me—"

I grab his hands to stop him from getting off the bed. "No, stop. I've been keeping up with all my treatments. Just give me a second." I stare at him and then I start laughing. Oh my gosh, am I still dreaming or is this happening?

"Pinch me."

A furrow appears between Logan's brows. "What?"

"Pinch me so I know I'm not dreaming."

That's all it takes. He pounces on me. "How about I do a lot more than pinch you?" he growls in my ear before dropping his lips and devouring my mouth. He nips my lips with his teeth. "This real enough for you?"

I can only moan in response.

"This real enough for you?" he slides a hand down from my neck to my breast and pinches my nipple in a way that sends a flood of wetness to my sex. "How about that?"

I arch off of the bed, a high-pitched "Yes," on my lips. I don't know if it's an affirmative to his question or and encouragement for him to do more.

Like the smart man he is, he takes it as both and then his hands are everywhere. Massaging. Pinching. Caressing. Teasing.

And I feel alive. So alive life is bursting from within me. I'm going to live. I'm going to live a long, full life full of laughter and Logan and happiness and love and—

Logan rolls us over in bed so that I'm laid flat on my back again, him over me like the devouring predator that he is.

But for once, he's missing the vacant look of desperation that always used to hover like a cloud over him, like any second he was ready to bolt the second you betrayed him, always on guard and ready for it.

Now, though, when he looks down at me, it's only with eyes full of love. Well, there's a fair amount of lust, too, but it's interwoven with love. And it's the most powerful emotion I've ever felt coming from him.

I'm so consumed by it, that I almost don't notice the shadow moving outside the window from the balcony.

Almost.

But Logan registers the stiffness of my body even before I've realized the shape of the shadow is a man.

And that man is holding a gun, pointed straight at us.

IT'S ADAM.

Adam's on our balcony with a gun.

The thought barely registers before Logan is off the bed and charging the balcony's double doors.

Wait—

How—?

No!

But there's no slow-motion like in the movies. It all happens in the blink of an eye.

Logan explodes through the balcony doors that open outwards, knocking Adam off balance.

I scream as the gun goes off. "Logan!"

The covers of the bed catch around me as I try to get to my feet and I almost fall off the bed trying to get to Logan. By the time I right myself, Logan and Adam are wrestling on the narrow balcony.

Where's the gun? Did Logan get shot? Does Adam still have the gun?

I run over to the doorway, looking for a vase or something else heavy to hit Adam with, but we're in Logan's bedroom in the castle and it's spare, almost no decoration. How the hell did Adam even get up to the balcony? We're three stories up. I know he does some free climbing but what the hell? And how the *hell* did he get here? I thought the police were going to arrest him.

By the time I grab Logan's laptop, the heaviest thing I can find, and make it back to the balcony, the fight has escalated.

Adam and Logan are both back on their feet, squaring off, right as the clouds darken overhead.

"You stole everything from me!" Adam howls. He

doesn't look well. He's in one of his fancy suits, but the shirt is buttoned off kilter and there are stains down the front of it.

"You're trash from the street who never deserved to lick the shit off the soles of my shoes and you think you get to win? You think some fucking rat off the street is going to best Adam fucking *Archer*? My grandfather shat in your grandparents' soup bowls and they ate it up and were *grateful*. But you—"

A sharp gut punch from Logan shuts Adam up but doesn't make him look any less mutinous. Fury pours off of him in waves as he glares back up at Logan and then lets out the roar of a wounded beast at the same time he charges.

But Logan's quick.

At the last moment, he feints left and then jerks out of the way to the right. But Adam's momentum continues forward. He's unable to readjust for the last minute move.

And he goes sailing right over the balcony in the spot where Logan was just standing.

Oh my g—!

The laptop I'm holding clatters to the carpeted rug at my feet as I run out onto the balcony.

But Logan holds out an arm to brace me, holding me back.

Which is when I hear Adam's panicked shouts.

"Help! *Heeeeeelp!*"

And I looked down to see that Adam is dangling from our balcony, holding on by just a few fingers to the stone railing.

The screams continue, jumping in pitch and octave until Adam is screeching in the range of a soprano. "Help! Oh gods, please. Help me! I'm *sorry*. I'm sorry for everything! I take it all back!"

Logan looks down at the flailing man in disgust, but only for a second before leaning over the waist-high railing to grasp Adam's wrist.

I'm only standing a couple of feet away from both of them and I see it—the instant the expression on Adam's face changes.

From panic to glee.

But I can't shout Logan's name fast enough.

Adam lets go of the balcony completely and grasps Logan's arm with both of his hands, yanking Logan off balance and pulling him further over the edge of the railing.

"I lost everything. And now so will you!"

Adam's a fucking maniac, jerking and twisting, trying to wrest Logan all the way over the edge of the railing. And it's working. Logan's cursing and struggling to get a hold on the railing, but inch by inch, he's going over.

Adam is winning. He's trying to take my Logan from me and he's winning.

"You son of a bitch!" I scream. And then I run forward, stick my leg through the railing so I can reach down to him, and kick Adam in his crazy, evil fucking face.

Adam tries to lunge for my leg with one of his hands, and that's his undoing.

He loses hold of Logan's arm.

And then he falls.

Strangely enough, this part does seem to go in slow motion.

Down and down he falls, arms wheeling in the air. I can't look away, somehow expecting something at the last minute to save him.

He's Adam Archer. Golden boy of the city. Sexiest Bachelor of the Year for three years running.

But no magical golden parachute appears beneath him.

He hits the ground, three stories down, as hard as any regular man would. And I know, even without running down the stairs to check, that he is just as dead as any other man would be after such a fall.

And I don't give a flying fuck.

I grab Logan around the waist and he grasps for the railing now that he has both arms free to steady himself. Together, we haul him back onto the balcony, where he collapses, heaving hard.

It's only then that I see he's bleeding. Not much, it looks like the bullet just grazed his cheek. The same one that's already scarred.

"Logan! Your face! Are you okay?"

He lifts a hand to his face and then looks at the blood on it. But then he just starts laughing.

He draws me into his arms, but that's obviously not enough, because soon he's dragging me into his lap and hugging me harder than I've ever been hugged before.

"It's over," he whispers into my hair. "Our happily ever after can finally begin."

EPILOGUE

Daphne
Five years later

"Isabella," I call, craning my head to peer into the bushes in the back garden. Her brother babbles on the blanket beside me, pulling up clumps of clover.

"I've got her," Logan's deep voice rings out a second before he appears with my girl on his shoulders. He has to duck to fit under the clematis covered archway, but then he pauses so Isabella can pick one of the purple flowers. They both drift my way so my daughter can present the blossom to me.

"Thank you. Baby, you didn't go into Daddy's office while he was working? You know you're supposed to stay out."

"I wanted to see Daddy." Isabella shrugs. "He said I could."

"It was fine." Logan sinks down next to me. "She sat on

my lap and didn't talk too much." He ruffles her hair and she gazes up at him adoringly.

She is such a Daddy's girl. Both of our kids have their dad's dark good looks, but Isabella has my mother's eyes.

"I thought you were on a call," I ask him quietly as the kids play together.

"I was." Logan lounges out beside me, his huge body taking over most of the blanket. He wriggles to get comfortable. I would've missed his sigh if I wasn't looking for it.

"Everything good?" I raise a brow. He knows better than to keep bad news from me.

"It's fine. I went over the latest numbers from the New Rome labs. St. James is happy."

"That's good." When I first learned of the deal Logan worked out with a shadow investor, I was skeptical. It seemed too good to be true. Unlimited funding for our full-time research? Logan wasn't sure either. "A deal with the devil," he called it.

But so far, it's worked out well. Just ask the other Battleman's patients who are in remission. Yeah, we have to have regular infusions, but we're able to live healthy, normal lives.

"St. James sends his regards. He'll be at the gala. No plus one." Logan grins suddenly. "I told him we'd help him find a date."

"You didn't." I can't imagine joking or teasing someone like St. James. He's my age, but so intimidating. "Maybe we should introduce him to Rachel. Whenever I call her, she complains she's too busy running Belladonna to have time to date."

Logan snorts. "They'd kill each other."

"Probably." I shake my head, imagining them meeting.

I'm about to joke about it when a few drops of water hit my arm.

Isabella runs up to us. "Mommy, it's raining."

"You grab her, I'll get Nathan and the blanket." Logan kisses me and we triage, racing inside ahead of the heavy summer downpour.

An hour later, Logan finds me in my mother's old room, which I've converted to my study. It has the best view of the gardens. I stare out the window, letting the rain lull me to peacefulness.

"Kids are asleep," my husband whispers in my ear.

"I was going to check the latest test results," I murmur. "But I might have a few minutes." I turn and ease up to tiptoe to twine my arms around his neck. "What do you think, Dr. Wulfe? Will this only take a few minutes?"

His answer is a growl. I laugh as he pounces. We make love under the open window until the storm recedes, leaving only the sound of dripping leaves and the heady fragrance of roses.

Hungry for more dark romance from Lee and Stasia?

FIND out what happens when Marcus, the king of the criminal underworld who always gets what he wants decides to capture the beautiful, innocent Cora, in his web. He'll give her all that her heart desires. Except for one thing. Her freedom. She's his to keep, and he's never letting her go.

Order INNOCENCE now so you don't miss out!

ALSO BY STASIA BLACK

Dark Contemporary Romances

Dark Mafia Series

Innocence

Awakening

Queen of the Underworld

Innocence Boxset

Beauty and the Rose Series

Beauty's Beast

Beauty and the Thorns

Beauty and the Rose

Taboo: a Dark Romance Boxset Collection

Love So Dark Duology

Cut So Deep

Break So Soft

Stud Ranch Series

The Virgin and the Beast: a Beauty and the Beast Tale

Hunter: a Snow White Romance

The Virgin Next Door: a Ménage Romance

Freebie

Indecent: A Taboo Proposal

SCI-FI ROMANCES

MARRIAGE RAFFLE SERIES

Theirs to Protect

Theirs to Pleasure

Theirs to Wed

Theirs to Defy

Theirs to Ransom

Marriage Raffle Boxset

DRACI ALIEN SERIES

My Alien's Obsession

My Alien's Baby

FREEBIE

Their Honeymoon

ALSO BY LEE SAVINO

Contemporary romance:

Beauty and the Lumberjacks: a dark reverse harem romance

Her Marine Daddy

Her Dueling Daddies

Royally Fucked - get free at www.leesavino.com

Paranormal & Sci fi romance:

The Alpha Series

The Draekon Series

The Berserker Series

ABOUT STASIA BLACK

STASIA BLACK grew up in Texas, recently spent a freezing five-year stint in Minnesota, and now is happily planted in sunny California, which she will never, ever leave.

She loves writing, reading, listening to podcasts, and has recently taken up biking after a twenty-year sabbatical (and has the bumps and bruises to prove it). She lives with her own personal cheerleader, aka, her handsome husband, and their teenage son. Wow. Typing that makes her feel old. And writing about herself in the third person makes her feel a little like a nutjob, but ahem! Where were we?

Stasia's drawn to romantic stories that don't take the easy way out. She wants to see beneath people's veneer and poke into their dark places, their twisted motives, and their deepest desires. Basically, she wants to create characters that make readers alternately laugh, cry ugly tears, want to toss their kindles across the room, and then declare they have a new FBB (forever book boyfriend).

Join Stasia's Facebook Group for Readers for access to deleted scenes, to chat with me and other fans and also get access to exclusive giveaways:
www.facebook.com/groups/stasiasbabes

facebook.com/stasiablackauthor

twitter.com/stasiawritesmut

instagram.com/stasiablackauthor

ABOUT LEE SAVINO

Lee Savino has grandiose goals but most days can't find her wallet or her keys so she just stays at home and writes. While she was studying creative writing at Hollins University, her first manuscript won the Hollins Fiction Prize.

She lives in the USA with her awesome family. You can find her on Facebook in the **Goddess Group** at www.facebook.com/groups/leesavino.

instagram.com/intothedarkromance